The Light Invisible

ROBERT HUGH BENSON

Foreword

Robert Hugh Benson's
The Light Invisible

The Light Invisible always seemed to me a beautiful book. It was in 1902 that Hugh began to write it, at Mirfield. He says that a book of stories of my own, *The Hill of Trouble*, put the idea into his head — but his stories have no resemblance to mine. Mine were archaic little romances, written in a style which a not unfriendly reviewer called "painfully kind," an epigram which always gave Hugh extreme amusement. His were modern, semi-mystical tales; ... it was the first book in which he spread his wings, and there is, I think, a fresh and ingenuous beauty about it, as of a delighted adventure among new faculties and powers.[1]

In this way Arthur C. Benson, Robert Hugh Benson's brother, re-called his impression of the present volume, *The Light Invisible*. For some reason, however, Hugh (as he was called) didn't share the generally favorable opinion of his own work. As Arthur further related:

... [H]e says that he personally came to dislike the book intensely from the spiritual point of view, as being feverish and sentimental, and designed unconsciously to quicken his own spiritual temperature. He adds that he thought the book mischievous, as laying stress on mystical intuition rather than Divine authority, and because it substituted the imagination for the soul. That is a dogmatic objection rather than a literary

objection; and I suppose he really disliked it
because it reminded him later of a time when he
was moving among shadows.

If such secondhand information is not enough to convince anyone, we have direct evidence from the pen of Father Benson himself. The Reverend C. C. Martindale, S.J., Benson's "official
biographer," quotes a letter that the author wrote, and then com-
ments at some length on his own theory as to why Father Benson
held the book so much in aversion.

I dislike, quite intensely, *The Light Invisible*, from
the spiritual point of view. I wrote it in moods of
great feverishness, and in what I now recognize as
a very subtle state of sentimentality; I was striving
to reassure myself of the truths of religion, and
assume, therefore, a positive and assertive tone that
was largely insincere.

According to Father Martindale, the above passage concludes
"by professing an entire disbelief that anyone *could* really like the
book, and had to be given a list of confessedly 'right people' who
did."[2] (Emphasis in the original.) Father Martindale conceived
the idea that Benson was "worried" that what became almost his
most popular book during his life had more success among Anglicans than Catholics.

It is more likely that Benson may have felt that he put a little too
much of his own self-doubt and personal struggle into the struc-
ture (as opposed to the theme) of the book. This seemed to be on
his mind from the very beginning. As Father Martindale relates:

Slightly nervous as to how his book's religious color
might affect the reputation or the feelings of the
Mirfield Community [a Protestant religious
community in which Father Benson spent time
before his conversion to Catholicism], he wrote a
complete volume of his own 'under an ingenious

pseudonym that I do not believe anyone will guess.'
He signed himself simply *Robert Benson*, reviving
the unused *R* and dropping *Hugh*. He even on one
occasion allowed it to be surmised that Mr. A. C.
Benson [his brother Arthur] had written the stories.[3]

This worry about self-revelation and, indeed, that of vocation,
consumed Benson. The question of vocation, Evelyn Waugh re-
marked in his "Introduction" to *Richard Raynal*, was a theme that
pervaded all of Benson's fiction and quite a bit of his non-fiction
as well. It was certainly a lifelong struggle, as Father Martindale
noted in his biography.

Benson often projected onto his fictional characters his own
struggle over vocation. Possibly Father Benson felt that in *The Light
Invisible* he did not put enough of a screen between himself and
his readers. The result, for someone as sensitive as Father Benson,
could have been seen as too much self-revelation. Paradoxically,
this self-revelation might account for the book's popularity.

Fr. Martindale's theory that Benson disliked *The Light Invisible*
because of its popularity among Anglicans, seems untenable.
Benson, while convinced that the fullness of truth could be found
in the Catholic Church alone, never denied that other Christian —
even non-Christian — churches and religions had at least some
measure of the truth. Many of his most sympathetic characters
(and some of the best drawn) are not Catholic. For the rest of his
life he expressed the greatest respect for the Church of England,
into which he had been born and in which he was raised.

So how are we to assess *The Light Invisible*? Is it worth reading,
or should we respect the author's apparent wishes and disregard
it? Aside from the fact that Father Benson never repudiated the
work and seems to have kept his seemingly adverse opinion of it
within a very small circle, its publication in this new edition should
speak for itself. After all, at least two of Benson's contemporaries,
one each from the Anglican and the Catholic communions, seemed

to agree that the book is well worth reading. We also, in addition, have some modern support for this work, and from a very discerning source.

Father John A. Hardon, S.J., "specially recommends" *The Light Invisible* in his book, *The Catholic Lifetime Reading Plan*.[4] The *Reading Plan* is a list of one hundred authors and their most important works designed to serve as a guide for Catholics seeking to enrich their cultural and spiritual lives. Father Hardon gives primacy of place to *The Light Invisible* among the books by Father Benson he recommends.

The Light Invisible marks the beginning of a delightful journey for any fan of serious, yet readable fiction. The collection is long enough to enjoy as a full meal in itself, yet short enough to whet the appetite for more — and there was more to come. Father Benson's conversion seems to have provided the inspiration for a series of rapidly written yet hard-hitting novels that, nonetheless, never fail to entertain. There were to be, ultimately, eighteen novels, two short story collections, four plays and a volume of poetry — to say nothing of his significant output of non-fiction — and all this in the space of barely ten years!

This works out to approximately three major books per year. And this in addition to lecture tours, preaching, missions, a large correspondence (handwritten), and attempting to organize a religious community — an impressive record for someone who seems to have been constantly worried whether he was doing what God wanted of him.

Had he not died at a relatively young age, Father Benson would doubtless have continued to struggle with this problem. Despite the fact that he excelled at writing fiction, he, like his contemporary Sir Arthur Conan Doyle, had a low opinion of his work that had the most popular effect. Father Martindale relates an amusing, yet revealing anecdote.

"Why don't you take more trouble over your novels?" a friend once asked him. "If a thing's worth doing at all, it's worth doing well."

"I totally disagree," he energetically exclaimed. "There are lots of things which are worth doing, but aren't in the least worth doing *well*."[5]

That remark strikingly reveals Father Benson's lifelong internal conflict over the problem of vocation. He seemed at times to be the quintessential amateur. With the sole exception of his priesthood, he never seemed to take things as seriously as other people thought he should. Part of this, of course, is the still-lingering attitude that clergy aren't supposed to do anything except pose in stained-glass attitudes for the benefit that their good example gives to others — an attitude that Father Benson continually lambasted. Many of his clergymen characters, Catholic and Protestant alike, seem to work very hard to make themselves caricatures by constantly posing and pontificating. They only succeed in sounding pompous — though never sanctimonious or hypocritical.

Father Benson was, in spite of his opinion that some things were not worth doing well — or, perhaps, because of it — a fairly good artist, an excellent organizer and administrator, a gifted orator and, of course, a superb writer, possibly even a great one. Treating only one thing as deserving of serious consideration — his vocation — he was able to achieve a high degree of natural unaffectedness in everything else. This came at the cost of a lifelong struggle to understand the only thing that truly mattered to him: his priesthood.

The Light Invisible is thus valuable not only because it is an excellent work of literature. It also reveals the author's lifelong struggle to determine precisely and fully what life is supposed to be about.

— *Michael D. Greaney, editor*

(Endnotes)

[1] A. C. Benson, *Hugh*. New York: Longmans, Green and Co., 1916, pp. 177 – 178.

[2] C. C. Martindale, S.J., *The Life of Monsignor Robert Hugh Benson, Vol. I*. London: Longmans, Green and Co., 1917, p. 178.

[3] *Ibid*., pp. 176-178.

[4] New York: Doubleday, 1989, p. 133.

[5] Martindale, Vol. I., p. 386.

Preface

My friend, whose talk I have reported in this book so far as I am able, would be the first to disclaim (as indeed he was always anxious to do) the role of an accredited teacher, other than that which his sacred office conferred on him.

All that he claimed (and this surely was within his rights) was to be at least sincere in his perceptions and expressions of spiritual truth. His power, as he was at pains to tell me, was no more than a particular development of a faculty common to all who possess a coherent spiritual life. To one Divine Truth finds entrance through laws of nature, to another through the medium of other sciences or arts; to my friend it presented itself in directly sensible forms. Had his experiences, however, even seemed to contravene Divine Revelation, he would have rejected them with horror: entire submission to the Divine Teacher upon earth, as he more than once told me, should normally precede the exercise of all other spiritual faculties. The deliberate reversal of this is nothing else than Protestantism in its extreme form, and must ultimately result in the extinction of faith.

For the rest, I can add nothing to his own words. It is of course more than possible that here and there I have failed to present his exact meaning; but at least I have taken pains to submit the book before publication to the judgment of those whose theological learning is sufficient to reassure me that at least I have not so far misunderstood my friend's words and tales, as to represent him as transgressing the explicit laws of ascetical, moral, mystical, or dogmatic theology.

To these counselors I must express my gratitude, as well as to others who have kindly given me the encouragement of their sympathy.

R. B.

Contents

The Green Robe

"To see a world in a grain of sand,
And a heaven in a wild flower;
Hold infinity in the palm of your hand,
And eternity in an hour."

Blake.

The old priest was silent for a moment. The song of a great bee boomed up out of the distance and ceased as the white bell of a flower beside me drooped suddenly under his weight.

"I have not made myself clear," said the priest again. "Let me think a minute." And he leaned back.

We were sitting on a little red tiled platform in his garden, in a sheltered angle of the wall. On one side of us rose the old irregular house, with its latticed windows, and its lichened roofs culminating in a bell turret; on the other I looked across the pleasant garden where great scarlet poppies hung like motionless flames in the hot June sunshine, to the tall living wall of yew, beyond which rose the heavy green masses of an elm in which a pigeon lamented, and above all a tender blue sky. The priest was looking out steadily before him with great childlike eyes that shone strangely in his thin face under his white hair. He was dressed in an old cassock that showed worn and green in the highlights.

"No," he said presently, "it is not faith that I mean; it is only an intense form of the gift of spiritual perception that God has given me; which gift indeed is common to us all in our measure. It is the faculty by which we verify for ourselves what we have received on authority and hold by faith. Spiritual life consists partly in exercising this faculty. Well, then, this form of that faculty God has been pleased to bestow upon me, just as He has been pleased to bestow on you a keen power of seeing and enjoying beauty where others perhaps see none; this is called artistic perception. It is no sort of credit to you or to me, any more than is the color of our eyes, or a faculty for mathematics, or an athletic body.

"Now in my case, in which you are pleased to be interested, the perception occasionally is so keen that the spiritual world appears to me as visible as what we call the natural world. In such moments, although I generally know the difference between the spiritual and the natural, yet they appear to me simultaneously, as if on the same plane. It depends on my choice as to which of the two I see the more clearly.

"Let me explain a little. It is a question of focus. A few minutes ago you were staring at the sky, but you did not see the sky. Your own thought lay before you instead. Then I spoke to you, and you started a little and looked at me; and you saw me, and your thought vanished. Now can you understand me if I say that these sudden glimpses that God has granted me, were as though when you looked at the sky, you saw both the sky and your thought at once, on the same plane, as I have said? Or think of it in another way. You know the sheet of plate glass that is across the upper part of the fireplace in my study. Well, it depends on the focus of your eyes, and your intention, whether you see the glass and the fireplate behind, or the room reflected in the glass. Now can you imagine what it would be to see them all at once? It is like that." And he made an outward gesture with his hands.

"Well," I said, "I scarcely understand. But please tell me, if you will, your first vision of that kind."

"I believe," he began, "that when I was a child the first clear vision came to me, but I only suppose it from my mother's diary. I have not the diary with me now, but there is an entry in it describing how I said I had seen a face look out of a wall and had run indoors from the garden; half frightened, but not terrified. But I remember nothing of it myself, and my mother seems to have thought it must have been a waking dream; and if it were not for what has happened to me since perhaps I should have thought it a dream too. But now the other explanation seems to me more likely. But the first clear vision that I remember for myself was as follows:

"When I was about fourteen years old I came home at the end of one July for my summer holidays. The pony cart was at the station to meet me when I arrived about four o'clock in the afternoon; but as there was a shortcut through the woods, I put my luggage into the cart, and started to walk the mile and a half by myself. The field path presently plunged into a pine wood, and I came over the slippery needles under the high arches of the pines with that intense ecstatic happiness of homecoming that some natures know so well. I hope sometimes that the first steps on the other side of death may be like that. The air was full of mellow sounds that seemed to emphasize the deep stillness of the woods, and of mellow lights that stirred among the shadowed greenness. I know this now, though I did not know it then. Until that day although the beauty and the color and sound of the world certainly affected me, yet I was not conscious of them, any more than of the air I breathed, because I did not then know what they meant. Well, I went on in this glowing dimness, noticing only the trees that might be climbed, the squirrels and moths that might be caught, and the sticks that might be shaped into arrows or bows.

"I must tell you, too, something of my religion at that time. It was the religion of most well-taught boys. In the foreground, if I may put it so, was morality: I must not do certain things; I must do certain other things. In the middle distance was a perception of God. Let me say that I realized that I was present to Him, but not that He was present to me. Our Savior dwelt in this middle distance, one whom I fancied ordinarily tender, sometimes stern. In the background there lay certain mysteries, sacramental and otherwise. These were chiefly the affairs of grown-up people. And infinitely far away, like clouds piled upon the horizon of a sea, was the invisible world of heaven whence God looked at me, golden gates and streets, now towering in their exclusiveness, now on Sunday evenings bright with a light of hope, now on wet mornings unutterably dreary. But all this was uninteresting to me. Here about me lay the tangible enjoyable world — this was reality: there in a misty picture lay religion, claiming, as I knew, my homage, but not my heart. Well; so I walked through these woods, a tiny human creature, yet greater, if I had only known it, than these giants of ruddy bodies and arms, and garlanded heads that stirred above me.

"My path presently came over a rise in the ground; and on my left lay a long glade, bordered by pines, fringed with bracken, but itself a folded carpet of smooth rabbit-cropped grass, with a quiet oblong pool in the center, some fifty yards below me.

"Now I cannot tell you how the vision began; but I found my-self, without experiencing any conscious shock, standing perfectly still, my lips dry, my eyes smarting with the intensity with which I had been staring down the glade, and one foot aching with the pressure with which I had rested upon it. It must have come upon me and enthralled me so swiftly that my brain had no time to re-flect. It was no work, therefore, of the imagination, but a clear and sudden vision. This is what I remember to have seen.

"I stood on the border of a vast robe; its material was green. A great fold of it lay full in view, but I was conscious that it stretched for almost unlimited miles. This great green robe blazed with em-broidery. There were straight lines of tawny work on either side which melted again into a darker green in high relief. Right in the center lay a pale agate stitched delicately into the robe with fine dark stitches; overhead the blue lining of this silken robe arched out. I was conscious that this robe was vast beyond conception, and that I stood as it were in a fold of it, as it lay stretched out on some unseen floor. But, clearer than any other thought, stood out in my mind the certainty that this robe had not been flung down and left, but that it clothed a Person. And even as this thought showed itself a ripple ran along the high relief in dark green, as if the wearer of the robe had just stirred. And I felt on my face the breeze of His motion. And it was this I suppose that brought me to myself.

"And then I looked again, and all was as it had been the last time I had passed this way. There was the glade and the pool and the pines and the sky overhead, and the Presence was gone. I was a boy walking home from the station, with dear delights of the pony and the air gun, and the wakings morning by morning in my own carpeted bedroom, before me.

"I tried, however, to see it again as I had seen it. No, it was not in the least like a robe; and above all where was the Person that wore it? There was no life about me, except my own, and the insect life that sang in the air, and the quiet meditative life of the growing things. But who was this Person I had suddenly perceived? And then it came upon me with a shock, and yet I was incredulous. It could not be the God of sermons and long prayers who demanded my presence Sunday by Sunday in His little church, that God Who watched me like a stern father. Why religion, I thought, told me that all was vanity and unreality, and that rabbits and pools and glades were nothing compared to Him who sits on the great white throne.

"I need not tell you that I never spoke of this at home. It seemed to me that I had stumbled upon a scene that was almost dreadful, that might be thought over in bed, or during an idle lonely morning in the garden, but must never be spoken of, and I can scarcely tell you when the time came that I understood that there was but one God after all."

The old man stopped talking. And I looked out again at the garden without answering him, and tried myself to see how the poppies were embroidered into a robe, and to hear how the chatter of the starlings was but the rustle of its movement, the clink of jewel against jewel, and the moan of the pigeon the creaking of the heavy silk, but I could not. The poppies flamed and the birds talked and sobbed, but that was all.

The Watcher

"Il faut d'abord rendre l'organe de la vision analogue et
semblable l'objet qu'il doit contempler."

Maeterlinck.

On the following day we went out soon after breakfast and
walked up and down a grass path between two yew
hedges; the dew was not yet off the grass that lay in shadow; and
thin patches of gossamer still hung like torn cambric on the yew
shoots on either side. As we passed for the second time up the path,
the old man suddenly stooped and pushing aside a dock leaf at the
foot of the hedge lifted a dead mouse, and looked at it as it lay
stiffly on the palm of his hand, and I saw that his eyes filled slowly
with the ready tears of old age.

"He has chosen his own resting place," he said. "Let him lie there.
Why did I disturb him?" — and he laid him gently down again;
and then gathering a fragment of wet earth he sprinkled it over the
mouse. "Earth to earth, ashes to ashes," he said, "in sure and certain hope" — and then he stopped; and straightening himself with
difficulty walked on, and I followed him.

"You seemed interested," he said, "in my story yesterday. Shall I
tell you how I saw a very different sight when I was a little older?"
And when I had told him how strange and attractive his story had
been, he began.

"I told you how I found it impossible to see again what I had
seen in the glade. For a few weeks, perhaps months, I tried now
and then to force myself to feel that Presence, or at least to see that
robe, but I could not, because it is the gift of God, and can no more
be gained by effort than ordinary sight can be won by a sightless
man; but I soon ceased to try.

"I reached eighteen years at last, that terrible age when the soul seems to have dwindled to a spark overlaid by a mountain of ashes — when blood and fire and death and loud noises seem the only things of interest, and all tender things shrink back and hide from the dreadful noonday of manhood. Someone gave me one of those shot-pistols that you may have seen, and I loved the sense of power that it gave me, for I had never had a gun. For a week or two in the summer holidays I was content with shooting at a mark, or at the level surface of water, and delighted to see the cardboard shattered, or the quiet pool torn to shreds along its mirror where the sky and green lay sleeping. Then that ceased to interest me, and I longed to see a living thing suddenly stop living at my will. Now," and he held up a deprecating hand, "I think sport is necessary for some natures. After all, the killing of creatures is necessary for man's food, and sport as you will tell me is a survival of man's delight in obtaining food, and it requires certain noble qualities of endurance and skill. I know all that, and I know further that for some natures it is a relief — an escape for humors that will otherwise find an evil vent. But I do know this — that for me it was not necessary.

"However, there was every excuse, and I went out in good faith one summer evening intending to shoot some rabbit as he ran to cover from the open field. I walked along the inside of a fence with a wood above me and on my left, and the green meadow on my right. Well, owing probably to my own lack of skill, though I could hear the patter and rush of the rabbits all round me, and could see them in the distance sitting up listening with cocked ears, as I stole along the fence, I could not get close enough to fire at them with any hope of what I fancied was success; and by the time that I had arrived at the end of the wood I was in an impatient mood.

"I stood for a moment or two leaning on the fence looking out of that pleasant coolness into the open meadow beyond; the sun had at that moment dipped behind the hill before me and all was in shadow except where there hung a glory about the topmost leaves of a beech that still caught the sun. The birds were beginning to come in from the fields, and were settling one by one in the wood behind me, staying here and there to sing one last line of melody. I could hear the quiet rush and then the sudden clap of a pigeon's wings as he came home, and as I listened I heard pealing out above all other sounds the long liquid song of a thrush somewhere above me. I looked up idly and tried to see the bird, and after a moment or two caught sight of him as the leaves of the beech parted in the breeze, his head lifted and his whole body vibrating with the joy of life and music. As someone has said, his body was one beating heart. The last radiance of the sun over the hill reached him and bathed him in golden warmth. Then the leaves closed again as the breeze dropped, but still his song rang out.

"Then there came on me a blinding desire to kill him. All the other creatures had mocked me and run home. Here at least was a victim, and I would pour out the sullen anger that had been gathering during my walk, and at least demand this one life as a substitute. Side by side with this I remembered clearly that I had come out to kill for food: that was my one justification. Side by side I saw both these things, and I had no excuse — no excuse.

"I turned my head every way and moved a step or two back to catch sight of him again, and, although this may sound fantastic and overwrought, in my whole being was a struggle between light and darkness. Every fiber of my life told me that the thrush had a right to live. Ah! he had earned it, if labor were wanting, by this very song that was guiding death towards him, but black sullen anger had thrown my conscience, and was now struggling to hold it down till the shot had been fired. Still I waited for the breeze, and then it came, cool and sweet smelling like the breath of a garden, and the leaves parted. There he sang in the sunshine, and in a moment I lifted the pistol and drew the trigger.

"With the crack of the cap came silence overhead, and after what seemed an interminable moment came the soft rush of something falling and the faint thud among last year's leaves. Then I stood half terrified, and stared among the dead leaves. All seemed dim and misty. My eyes were still a little dazzled by the bright background of sunlit air and rosy clouds on which I had looked with such intensity, and the space beneath the branches was a world of shadows. Still I looked a few yards away, trying to make out the body of the thrush, and fearing to hear a struggle of beating wings among the dry leaves.

"And then I lifted my eyes a little, vaguely. A yard or two beyond where the thrush lay was a rhododendron bush. The blossoms had fallen and the outline of dark, heavy leaves was unrelieved by the slightest touch of color. As I looked at it, I saw a face looking down from the higher branches.

"It was a perfectly hairless head and face, the thin lips were parted in a wide smile of laughter, there were innumerable lines about the corners of the mouth, and the eyes were surrounded by creases of merriment. What was perhaps most terrible about it all was that the eyes were not looking at me, but down among the leaves; the heavy eyelids lay drooping, and the long, narrow, shining slits showed how the eyes laughed beneath them. The forehead sloped quickly back, like a cat's head. The face was the color of earth, and the outlines of the head faded below the ears and chin into the gloom of the dark bush There was no throat, or body or limbs so far as I could see. The face just hung there like a down-turned Eastern mask in an old curiosity shop. And it smiled with sheer delight, not at me, but at the thrush's body. There was no change of expression so long as I watched it, just a silent smile of pleasure petrified on the face. I could not move my eyes from it.

"After what I suppose was a minute or so, the face had gone. I did not see it go, but I became aware that I was looking only at leaves.

"No; there was no outline of leaf, or play of shadows that could possibly have taken the form of a face. You can guess how I tried to force myself to believe that that was all; how I turned my head this way and that to catch it again; but there was no hint of a face.

"Now, I cannot tell you how I did it; but although I was half beside myself with fright, I went forward towards the bush and searched furiously among the leaves for the body of the thrush; and at last I found it, and lifted it. It was still limp and warm to the touch. Its breast was a little ruffled, and one tiny drop of blood lay at the root of the beak below the eyes, like a tear of dismay and sorrow at such an unmerited, unexpected death.

"I carried it to the fence and climbed over, and then began to run in great steps looking now and then awfully at the gathering gloom of the wood behind, where the laughing face had mocked the dead. I think, looking back as I do now, that my chief instinct was that I could not leave the thrush there to be laughed at, and that I must get it out into the clean, airy meadow When I reached the middle of the meadow I came to a pond which never ran quite dry even in the hottest summer. On the bank I laid the thrush down, and then deliberately but with all my force dashed the pistol into the water; then emptied my pockets of the cartridges and threw them in too.

"Then I turned again to the piteous little body, feeling that at least I had tried to make amends. There was an old rabbit hole near, the grass growing down in its mouth, and a tangle of web and dead leaves behind. I scooped a little space out among the leaves, and then laid the thrush there; gathered a little of the sandy soil and poured it over the body, saying, I remember, halt unconsciously, 'Earth to earth, ashes to ashes, in sure and certain hope' — and then I stopped, feeling I had been a little profane, though I do not think so now. And then I went home.

"As I dressed for dinner, looking out over the darkening meadow where the thrush lay, I remember feeling happy that no evil thing could mock the defenseless dead out there in the clean meadow where the wind blew and the stars shone down."

We reached in our going to and fro up the yew path a little seat at the end standing back from the path. Opposite us hung a crucifix, with a penthouse over it, that the old man had put up years before. As he did not speak I turned to him, and saw that he was looking steadily at the Figure on the Cross; and I thought how He who bore our griefs and carried our sorrows was one with the heavenly Father, without whom not even a sparrow falls to the ground.

The Blood Eagle

"And this I know: whether the one True Light
Kindle to Lore or Wrath — consume me quite,
One glimpse of It within the Tavern caught
Better than in the Temple lost outright."

Omar Khayyam.

One night when I went to my room I found in a little shelf near the window a book, whose title I now forget, describing the far-off days when the religion of Christ and of the gods of the north strove together in England. I read this for an hour or two before I went to sleep, and again as I was dressing on the following morning, and spoke of it at breakfast.

"Yes," said the old man, "that was one of my father's books. I remember reading it when I was a boy. I believe it is said to be very ill informed and unscientific in these days. My parents used to think that all religions except Christianity were of the devil. But I think St. Paul teaches us a larger hope than that."

He said nothing more at the time; but in the course of the morning, as I was walking up and down the raised terrace that runs under the pines beside the drive, I saw the priest coming towards me with a book in his hand. He was a little dusty and flushed.

"I went to look for something that I thought might interest you, after what you said at breakfast," he began, "and I have found it at last in the loft."

We began to walk together up and down.

"A very curious thing happened to me," he said, "when I was a boy. I remember telling my father of it when I came home, and it remained in my mind. A few years afterwards an old professor was staying with us; and after dinner one night, when we had been talking about what you were speaking of at breakfast, my father made me tell it again, and when I had finished the professor asked me to write it down for him. So I wrote it in this book first; and then made a copy and sent it to him. The book itself is a kind of irregular diary in which I used to write sometimes. Would you care to hear it?"

When I had told him I should like to hear the story, he began again.

"I must first tell you the circumstances. I was about sixteen years old. My parents had gone abroad for the holidays, and I went to stay with a school friend of mine at his home not far from Ascot. We used to take our lunch with us sometimes on bright days — for it was at Christmas time — and go off for the day over the heather. You must remember that I was only a schoolboy at the time, so I daresay I exaggerated or elaborated some of the details a little, but the main facts of the story you can rely upon. Shall we sit down while I read it?"

Then when we had seated ourselves on a bench that stood at the end of the terrace, with the old house basking before us in the hot sunshine, he began to read.

"About six o'clock in the evening of one of the days towards the end of January, Jack and I were still wandering on high, heathy ground near Ascot. We had walked all day and had lost ourselves; but we kept going in as straight a line as we could, knowing that in time we should strike across a road. We were rather tired and si-lent; but suddenly Jack uttered an exclamation, and then pointed out a light across the heath. We stood a moment to see if it moved, but it remained still.

"'What is it?' I asked. 'There can be no house near here.'

"'It's a broom squire's cottage, I expect,' said Jack.

"I asked what that meant.

"'Oh! I don't know exactly,' said Jack; 'they're a kind of Gypsies.'

"We stumbled on across the heather, while the light grew steadily nearer. The moon was beginning to rise, and it was a clear night, one of those windless, frosty nights that sometimes come after a wet autumn. Jack plunged at one place into a hidden ditch, and I heard the crackling of ice as he scrambled out.

"'Skating tomorrow, by Jove,' he said.

"As we got closer I began to see that we were approaching a copse of firs; the heather began to get shorter. Then, as I looked at the light, I saw there was a fixed outline of a kind of house out of which it shone. The window apparently was an irregular shape, and the house seemed to be leaning against a tall fir on the outskirts of the copse. As we got quite close, our feet noiseless on the soft heather, I saw that the house was built altogether round the fir, which served as a kind of central prop. The house was made of wattled boughs, and thatched heavily with heather.

"I felt more and more anxious about it, for I had never heard of 'broom squires,' and also, I confess, a little timid for the place was lonely, and we were only two boys. I was leading now, and presently reached the window and looked in.

"The walls inside were hung with blankets and clothes to keep the wind out; there was a long old settle in one corner, the floor was carpeted with branches and blankets apparently, and there was an opening opposite, partly closed by a wattled hurdle that leaned against it. Half sitting and half lying on the settle, was an old woman with her face hidden. An oil lamp hung from one of the branches of the fir that helped to form the roof. There was no sign of any other living thing in the place. As I looked Jack came up behind and spoke over my shoulder.

"'Can you tell us the way to the nearest high road?' he asked.

"The old woman sat up suddenly, with a look of fright on her face. She was extraordinarily dirty and ill-kempt. I could see in the dim light of the lamp that she had a wrinkled old face, with sunken dark eyes, white eyebrows, and white hair; and her mouth began to mumble as she looked at us. Presently she made a violent gesture to wave us from the window.

"Jack repeated the question, and the old woman got up and hobbled quietly and crookedly to the door, and in a moment she had come round close to us. I then saw how very small she was. She could not have been five feet tall, and was very much bent. I must say again that I felt very uneasy and startled with this terrifying old creature close to me and peering up into my face. She took me by the coat and with her other hand beckoned quickly away in every direction. She seemed to be warning us away from the copse, but still she said nothing.

"Jack grew impatient.

"'Deaf old fool!' he said in an undertone, and then loudly and slowly, 'Can you tell us the way to the nearest highroad?'

"Then she seemed to understand, and pointed vigorously in the direction from which we had come.

"'Oh! Nonsense,' said Jack, 'we've come from there. Come on this way,' he said, 'we can't spend all night here.' And then he turned the side of the little house and disappeared into the copse.

"The old woman dropped my coat in a moment, and began to run after Jack, and I went round the other side of the house and saw Jack moving in front, for the firs were sparse at the edge of the wood, and the moonlight filtered through them. The old woman, I saw as I turned into the wood, had stopped, knowing she could not catch us, and was standing with her hands stretched out, and a curious sound, half cry and half sob, came from her. I was a little uneasy, because we had not treated her with courtesy, and stopped, but at that moment Jack called.

"'Come on,' he said, 'we're sure to find road at the end of this.'

"So I went on.

"Once I turned and saw the little old woman standing as before; and as I looked between the trees she lifted one hand to her mouth and sent a curious whistling cry after us, that somehow frightened me. It seemed too loud for one so small.

"As we went on the wood grew darker. Here and there in an open patch there lay a white splash of moonlight on the fir needles, and great dim spaces lay round us. Although the wood stood on high ground, the trees grew so thickly about us that we could see nothing of the country round. Now and then we tripped on a root, or else caught in a bramble, but it seemed to me that we were following a narrow path that led deeper and deeper into the heart of the wood. Suddenly Jack stopped and lifted his hand.

"'Hush!' he said.

"I stopped too, and we listened breathlessly. Then in a moment more, "'Hush!' he said, 'something's coming,' and he jumped out of the path behind a tree, and I followed him.

"Then we heard a scuffling in front of us and a grunting, and some big creature came hurrying down the path. As it passed us I looked, almost terrified out of my mind, and saw that it was a huge pig; but the thing that held me breathless and sick was that there ran nearly the whole length of its back a deep wound, from which the blood dripped. The creature, grunting heavily, tore down the path towards the cottage, and presently the sound of it died away. As I leaned against Jack, I could feel his arm trembling as it held the tree.

"'Oh,' he said in a moment, 'we must get out of this. Which way, which way?'

"But I had been still listening, and held him quiet.

"'Wait,' I said, 'there is something else.'

"Out of the wood in front of us there came a panting, and the soft sounds of hobbling steps along the path. We crouched lower and watched. Presently the figure of a bent old man came in sight, making his way quickly along the path. He seemed startled and out of breath. His mouth was moving, and he was talking to himself in a low voice in a complaining tone, but his eyes searched the wood from side to side.

"As he came quite close to us, as we lay hardly daring to breathe, I saw one of his hands that hung in front of him, opening and shutting; and that it was stained with what looked black in the moonlight. He did not see us, as by now we were hidden by a great bramble bush, and he passed on down the path; and then all was silent again.

"When a few minutes had passed in perfect stillness, we got up and went on, but neither of us cared to walk in the path down which those two terrible dripping things had come; and we went stumbling over the broken ground, keeping a parallel course to the path for about another two hundred yards. Jack had begun to recover himself, and even began to talk and laugh at being frightened at a pig and an old man. He told me afterwards that he had not seen the old man's hand.

"Then the path began to lead uphill. At this point I suddenly stopped Jack.

"'Do you see nothing?' I asked.

"Now I scarcely remember what I said or did. But this is what my friend told me afterwards. Jack said there was nothing but a little rising ground in front, from which the trees stood back.

"'Do you see nothing on the top of the mound? Out in the open, where the moonlight falls on her?'

"Jack told me afterwards that he thought I had gone suddenly mad, and grew frightened himself.

"'Do you not see a woman standing there? She has long yellow hair in two braids; she has thick gold bracelets on her bare arms. She has a tunic, bound by a girdle, and it comes below her knees: and she has red jewels in her hair, on her belt, on her bracelets; and her eyes shine in the moonlight: and she is waiting, — waiting for that which has escaped.'

"Now Jack tells me that when I said this I fell flat on my face, with my hands stretched out, and began to talk: but he said he could not understand a word I said. He himself looked steadily at the rising ground, but there was nothing to be seen there: there were the fir trees standing in a circle round it, and a bare space in the middle, from which the heather was gone, and that was all. This mound would be about fifteen yards from us.

"I lay there, said Jack, a few minutes, and then sat up and looked about me. Then I remembered for myself that I had seen the pig and the old man, but nothing more: but I was terrified at the re- membrance, and insisted upon our striking out a new course through the wood, and leaving the mound to our left. I did not know myself why the mound frightened me, but I dared not go near it. Jack wisely did not say anything more about it until after- wards. We presently found our way out of the copse, struck across the heath for another half mile or so, and then came across a road which Jack knew, and so we came home.

"When we told our story, and Jack, to my astonishment, had added the part of which I myself had no remembrance, Jack's father did not say very much; but he took us next day to identify the place. To our intense surprise the house of the broom squire was gone; there were the trampled branches round the tree, and the smoked branch from which the oil lamp had hung and the ashes of a wood fire outside the house, but no sign of the old man or his wife. As we went along the path, now in the cheerful frosty sunshine, we found dark splashes here and there on the brambles, but they were dry and colorless. Then we came to the mound.

"I grew uneasy again as we came to it, but was ashamed to show my fear in the broad daylight.

"On the top we found a curious thing, which Jack's father told us was one of the old customs of the broom squires, that no one was altogether able to explain. The ground was shoveled away, so as to form a kind of sloping passage downwards into the earth. The passage was not more than five yards long; and at the end of it, just where it was covered by the ground overhead, was a sort of altar, made of earth and stones beaten flat; and plastered into its surface were bits of old china and glass. But what startled us was to find a dark patch of something which had soaked deep into the ground before the altar. It was still damp."

When the old man had read so far, he laid down the book.

"When I told all this to the Professor," he said, "he seemed very deeply interested. He told us, I remember, that the wound on the pig identified the nature of the sacrifice that the old man had begun to offer. He called it a 'blood eagle,' and added some details which I will not disgust you with. He said too that the broom squire had confused two rites — that only human sacrifices should be offered as 'blood eagles.' In fact it all seemed perfectly familiar to him: and he said more than I can either remember or verify."

"And the woman on the rising ground?" I asked.

"Well," said the old man, smiling, "the Professor would not listen to my evidence about that. He accepted the early part of the story, and simply declined to pay any attention to the woman. He said I had been reading Norse tales, or was dreaming. He even hinted that I was romancing. Under other circumstances this method of treating evidence would be called 'Higher Criticism,' I believe."

"But it's all a brutal and disgusting worship," I said.

"Yes, yes," said the old man, "very brutal and disgusting; but is it not very much higher and better than the Professor's faith? He was only a skilled Ritualist after all, you see."

Over the Gateway

"— For faith, that, when my need is sore,
Gleams from a partly-open door,
And shows the firelight on the floor —"

A Canticle of Common Things

We were sitting together one morning in the common sitting room in the center of the house. There had been a fall of rain during the night, and it was thought better that the old man should not sit in the garden until the sun had dried the earth — so we sat indoors instead, but with the great door wide open, that looked on to a rectangle of lawn that lay before the house. Once a drive had led to this door through a gate with pedestals and stone balls, that stood exactly opposite, about fifteen yards away, but the drive had long been grassed over; although even now it showed faintly under two slight ridges in the grass that ran from the gate to the door. Otherwise the lawn was enclosed by low old brick wall, almost hidden by a wealth of ivy, against which showed in rich masses of color the heads of purple and yellow irises and tawny wallflowers.

The old man had been silent at breakfast. He had offered the Holy Sacrifice as usual that morning in the little chapel upstairs, and I had noticed even at the time that he seemed preoccupied: and at breakfast he had talked very little, letting every subject drop as I suggested it; and I had understood at last that his thoughts were far away in the past; and I did not wish to trouble him.

We were sitting in two tall carved chairs at the doorway, his feet were wrapped in a rug, and his eyes were looking steadily and mournfully out across towards the ironwork gate in the wall. Tall grasses of the patch of uncut meadow outside leaned against it or pushed their feathery heads through it; and I saw presently that the priest was looking at the gate, letting his eyes rove over every detail of climbing plant, iron work and the old brickwork — and not, as I had at first thought, merely gazing into the dim distances of the years behind him.

Suddenly he broke the long silence.

"Did I ever tell you," he asked, "about what I saw out there in the garden? It looks ordinary enough now: yet I saw there what I suppose I shall never see again on this side of death, or at least not until I am in the very gate of death itself."

I too looked out at the gate. The atmosphere was full of that "clear shining after rain" of which King David sang — it was air made visible and radiant by the union of light and water, those two most joyous creatures of God. A great chestnut tree blotted out all beyond the gate.

"Tell me if you can," I said. "You know how I love to hear those stories."

"Years ago, as perhaps you know, not long after my ordination I was working in London. My father lived here then, as his father before him. That coat of arms in the center of that iron gate was put up by him soon after he succeeded to the property. I used to come down here now and then for a breath of country air. I hardly remember any pleasure so keen as the pleasure of coming into this glorious country air out of the smoke and noise of London — or of lying awake at night with the rustle of the pines outside my window instead of the ceaseless human tumult of the town.

"Well, I came down here once, suddenly, on a summer evening, bearing heavy news. I need not go into details; it would be useless to do that — but it will be enough to say that the news did not personally affect me or my family. It was a curious series of circumstances that led me to be the bearer of such news at all — but it was to a lady who happened by the merest chance to be staying with my family. I scarcely knew her at all — in fact I had only seen her once before. The news had come to my ears in London, and I had heard that the one whom it most concerned did not know it — and that they dared not write or telegraph. I volunteered of course to take the news myself.

"It was with a very heavy heart that I walked up from the station — the road seemed intolerably short. I may say that I knew that the news would be heartbreaking to her who had to hear it. I came in by the gate at the end of the avenue —" (he waved his hand round to the right) "and passed right down to the back of the house, behind us. This door by which we are sitting had been the front door, but the drive had just been turfed over, and we used the door at the back instead, and this lawn here was very much as you see it now, only the drive still showed plainly like a long narrow grave across the grass.

"As I came in through the door at the back, she was coming out, with a book and a basket-chair to sit in the garden. My heart gave a terrible throb of pain — for I knew that by the time my business was done there would be no thought of a quiet evening in the garden, and that look of serene happiness would be wiped out of her face — and all through what I had to say. For a moment she did not recognize me in the dark entry and stood back as I came in and then,

"'Why it is you,' she said; 'you have come home. I did not know you were expected.'

"I breathed a moment steadily to recover myself.

"'I was not expected,' I said; and then, after a moment: 'May I speak to you?'

"'Speak to me? Why, certainly. The garden or here?'

"'In here,' I answered, and went past her and pushed open the door into this room.

"She came past me, and stood here by the door still holding the book, with her finger between the leaves.

"Now you are wondering, I expect, why I did not get some other woman to break the news to her. Well, I had debated that ever since I had volunteered to be the bearer of these tidings: and partly because I was afraid of being cowardly — call it pride if you will — and partly for other reasons which I need not mention, I felt I was bound to fulfill my promise literally. It might be, I thought too, that she would prefer the news to be known by as few people as possible. At least, whether I judged rightly or wrongly, here was my task before me.

"She stood there," the old man went on, pointing to the door post on the right, "and I here," and he pointed a yard further back, "and the door was wide open as it is now, and the fragrant evening air poured past us into the room. Her face would be partly in shadow; but in her eyes there was just a dawning wonder at my abruptness, with perhaps the faintest tinge of anxiety, but no more.

"'I have come,' I said slowly, looking out into the garden, 'on a very hard errand.' I could not go on. I turned and looked at her. Ah! The anxiety had deepened a little. 'And — and it concerns you and your happiness.' I looked again, and I remember how her face had changed. Her lips were a little open, and her eyes shone wide open, half in shadow and half in light, and there were new and terrible little lines on her forehead. And then I told her.

"It was done in a sentence or two and when I looked again her lips had closed and her hand had clenched itself into the molding of the door post. I can see her rings now blazing in the light that poured over the chestnut tree (it was lower then) into the room. Then her lips moved once or twice — her hand unclenched itself hesitatingly — and she went steadily across the room. There was a great sofa there then, and when she reached it she threw herself face downwards across the arm and back.

"And I waited at the doorway, looking out at the iron gate. Sorrow was new to me then. I had not learned to understand it then, or to be quiet under it. And as I looked I knew only that there was a terrible struggle going on in the room behind. There in front of me was a garden full of peace and sweetness and the soft glow of sunset light; and there behind me was something very like hell — and I stood between the living and the dead.

"Then I remembered that I was a priest, and ought to be able to say something — just a word of the Divine message that the Savior brought — but I could not. I felt I was in deep waters. Even God seemed far away, intolerably serene and aloof; and I longed with all my power for a human person to pray and to bear a little of that strife behind me, from which I felt separated by so wide a gulf. And then God gave me the clear vision again.

"You see the iron gate," the old man went on, pointing. "Well, right between those posts, but a little above them, outlined clearly against the chestnut tree, beyond, was the figure of a man.

"Now I do not know how to explain myself, but I was conscious that across this material world of light and color there cut a plane of the spiritual world, and that where the planes crossed I could look through and see what was beyond. It was like smoke cutting across a sunbeam. Each made the other visible.

"Well, this figure of a man, then, was kneeling in the air, that is the only way I can describe it — his face was turned towards me, but upwards. Now the most curious thing that struck me at the time was that he was, as it were, leaning at a sharp angle to one side; but it did not appear to be grotesque. Instead the world seemed tilted; the chestnut tree was out of the perpendicular; the wall out of the horizontal. The true level was that of the man.

"I know this sounds foolish, but it showed me how the world of spirits was the real world, and the world of sense comparatively unreal, just as the sorrow of the woman behind me was more real than the beams overhead.

"And again, compared with the kneeling figure, the chestnut tree and the gate seemed unsubstantial and shadowy. I know that men who see visions tell us that it is usually the other way. All I can say is that it was not so with me. This figure was kneeling, as I have said; his robe streamed away behind him — a great cloak — drawn tightly back from the shoulders, as if he were battling with a strong wind — the Wind of Grace, I suppose, that always blows from the Throne. His arms were stretched out in front of him, but opened sufficiently to let me see his face; and his face will be with me till I die, and please God afterwards. It was beardless, and bore the unmistakable character of a priest's face.

"Now you know how close the intensest pain and the intensest joy lie together. Their lines so nearly meet. In this man's face they did meet. Anguish and ecstasy were one. His eyes were open, his lips parted. I could not tell whether he was old or young. His face was ageless, as the faces of all are who look upon Him who inhabits eternity. He was praying. I can say no more than that. He had opened his heart to this woman's sorrow. He had made it his own: and it met there; in petition if you wish to call it so, or in resignation if you prefer that name for it, or in adoration — you may call it what you will — all that is true, but each is inadequate — but that sorrow met there with his own purified will, which itself had become one with the eternal will of God. I tell you I know it.

"I looked at him, and in my ears was sobbing from the room behind; but as I looked the glory of anguish deepened on his face, and the sobbing behind me slackened and ceased, and I heard a whispering and the name of God and of His Son, and then the sight before me had passed; and there stood the chestnut tree again as real and as beautiful as before; and when I turned the woman was standing up, and the light of conquest was in her eyes.

"She held out her hand to me, and I stooped and kissed it, but I dared not take it in my own, for she had been in heavenly places. I had seen her sorrow carried and laid before the throne of God by one greater than either of us, and something of his glory rested upon her."

The old man's voice ceased. When I turned to look at him he was looking steadily again at the iron gate in the wall, and his eyes were shining like the radiant air outside. "I do not know," he said in a moment, "whether she is alive or dead, but I offered the Holy Sacrifice this morning for her peace in either state."

Poena Damni

All their sins stand before them, and produce in their essences
remorse, eternal despair and a hostile will against God. For such a
soul there is no remedy. It cannot come into the light of God....
Even if St. Peter had left many thousand keys upon earth, not a
single one of them could open Heaven for it."

A German Mystic

We were sitting at dinner one evening when the priest,
who had been talkative, seemed to fall into a painful
train of thought that silenced him. He grew more and more ill at
ease, and was obviously relieved when I threw my cigarette away
and he was able to propose a move to the next room. Presently his
distress seemed to pass; and then, as we sat near the fireplace, he
explained himself.

"'I must ask your pardon," he said, "but somehow I fell into a
very dreadful train of thought. It was suggested to me, I think, by
the red lamp on the table and the evening light through the windows, and the silver and glass. (You know the power of associa-
tion!) I went through one of the most fearful moments of my life
under just those circumstances."

I was silent, as the priest seemed to have more to say.

"It has affected my nerves," he said, "and it would be rather a
relief to tell you. Would you mind if I did so? "

On my assurance that it would greatly interest me, he began.

"It is a fashion among those who do not really accept Revelation as revelation to believe in a kind of Universalism. Quite apart
from authority, this doctrine contravenes, as you of course know,
the reality of man's free will. The incident of which I wish to tell
you concerns the way in which I first caught a glimpse of that for

myself.

"A good many years ago I made the acquaintance of a man in the West of England, under circumstances that I need not describe further than saying that he seemed to have confidence in me. He asked me to stay with him in his country house, and I went down from London for the inside of a week. I found him living the usual country life, fishing and so forth; for it was summer when I visited him. It was a fine old house that he lived in, surrounded by coverts. He had a charming wife and two or three children, and at first I thought him extremely happy and contented.

"Then I thought that I noticed that things were not so well with him. The cottages on his estate were ill-cared for, and that is always a bad sign. From one or two small signs, such as you can guess, I found that the tone among his servants was not what it should be; and one or two horrid pieces of cruelty came under my notice. I know this sounds as if I were a sort of spy, greedy for information; but all that I can say is, that these signs were unmistakable and obvious, and came to me, of course, unsought and unexpected. Then I saw that his domestic relations were not right. I do not know how else to describe all this than by saying that there seemed a kind of blight upon his surroundings. Nothing was absolutely wrong, and yet all was just wrong.

"At first I thought that I myself was depressed or jaundiced in some way; but at last I could not continue to believe that; and on the Friday of my stay, the last day, I became finally certain that something was horribly wrong with the man himself. Then that evening he opened his heart to me, so far as it was possible for him to do so.

"His wife, with the two daughters, had left us after dessert and gone into the garden, and we remained in the dining room. The windows looked to the west, across a smooth sloping lawn, with the lake at the end; beyond that rose up a delicate birch wood, and beyond that again a soft green sky, where the sun had set, deepening into a liquid evening blue overhead, in which a star or two glimmered. I could see, as I looked out, the white figures of his wife and daughters against the shining surface of the lake at the end of the lawn.

"After he had lit his cigarette, and had a glass or two of wine, suddenly he opened his heart to me, and told me an appalling story that I could not tell you. I sat and watched his strong sinewy hand rise and fall with the cigarette, under the red lamplight; I glanced at his quiet well-bred face with the downcast eyes and the long mustache, and I wondered whether it was possible really for such a tale to be true but he spoke with a restrained conviction that left no room for doubt. What I gathered from the story was this; — that he had identified himself, his whole world, his whole life practically, with the cause of Satan. I could not detect as he talked that he had ever seriously attempted to detach himself from that cause. It has been said that a saint is one who always chooses the better of the two courses open to him at every step; so far as I could see this man had always chosen the worse of the two courses. When he had done things that you and I would think right, he had always done them for some bad reason. He had been continuously aware, too, of what was happening. I do not think that I have ever heard such a skillful self analysis. Now and then, as I saw the gulf of despair towards which his talk was leading, I interrupted him, suggesting alleviations of the horror — suggesting that he was pessimistic — that he had acted often under misconceptions — and the like; but he always met me with a quiet answer that silenced me. In fact," said the priest, who was beginning to tremble a little, "I have never thought it possible that a heart could be so corrupt and yet retain so much knowledge and feeling.

"When he had finished his story he looked at me for a moment, and then said:

"'Lately I have seen what I have lost, and what I shall lose; and I have told you this to ask if the Christian Gospel has any hope for such as I am.'

"Of course I answered as a Christian priest must answer, for I honestly thought that here was the greatest miracle of God's grace that I had ever seen. When I had finished I lifted my eyes from the cloth and looked up. His fingers, while I was speaking, had been playing with an apostle spoon, but as I looked up he looked up too, and our eyes met."

As the priest said this, he got up, and leaned his head against the high oak mantelpiece, and was silent a moment. Then he went on:

"God forgive me if I was wrong — if I am wrong now — but this is what I think I saw.

"Out of his eyes looked a lost soul. As a symbol, or a sign, too, his eyes shone suddenly with that dull red light that you may see sometimes in a dog's eyes. It was the *poena damni* of which I had read, which shone there. It was true, as he had said, that he was seeing clearly what he had lost and would lose; it was the gate of heaven opening to one who could not enter in. It was the chink of light under the door to one who cried, 'Lord, Lord, open to me,' but through the door there came that answer, 'I know you not.' Ah! it was not that he had never known before what God was, and His service and love; it was just his condemnation that he had known: that he had seen, not once or twice but again and again, the two ways, and had, not once nor twice but again and again, chosen the worse of those two; and now he was powerless.

"I tell you I saw this for a moment. There was this human face, so well-bred, with its delicate lines, looking almost ethereal in the soft red light of the lamp: behind him, between the windows hung a portrait of an ancestor, some old Caroline divine in ruff and bands. Through the windows was that sweet glory of evening — with the three figures by the lake. Here, between us, was the delicate soothing luxury of cleanliness and coolness and refreshment, such as glass and silver and fruit suggest: and there for one second in this frame of beauty and peace looked the eyes of one who desired even a drop of living water to cool his tongue, for he was tormented in a flame.

"And I saw all this; and then the room began to swim and whirl, and the table to tilt and sway, and I fell, I suppose, forward, and sank down on to the floor. When I recovered there were the men in the room, and the anxious face of my host looking down on me.

"I had to return to town the next morning. I wrote to him a long letter the following week, saying that I had been ill on the evening on which he had given me his confidence: and that I had not said all that I could say: and I went on, giving the lie to what I had thought I had seen, speaking to him as I should speak to any soul who was weary of sin and desired God.

"Indeed I thought it most possible, as I wrote the letter, that I had had a horrible delusion; and that all could be well with him. I got an answer of a few lines, saying that he must apologize for having troubled me with such a story; adding that he had greatly exaggerated his own sin; that he too had been over-excited and unwell: and that he too trusted in a God of Love — and begging me not to refer to the conversation again."

The priest sat down again.

"Now you may of course accept this version of it, if you will. I only would to God that I could too."

"Consolatrix Afflictorum"

"Should it be burdensome for thee ... she will for thy sake
herself raise me up when I chance to fall, and console me when
sorrowing."

St. Leander of Seville.

The following letter will explain itself. The original was read
to me by my friend on one of those days during my stay
with him; and he allowed me, at my request, to make a copy. The
sermon referred to in the first sentence of the letter was preached
in a foreign watering place on Christmas Day.

"VILLA —

"Reverend and Dear Sir,

"December 29, 18 —

"I listened with great attention to your sermon on Christmas
Day; I am getting on in years, and I am an invalid; so you will
understand that I have few friends — and I think none who would
not think me mad if I told them the story that I am proposing to
tell you. For many years I have been silent on this subject; since it
always used to be received with incredulity. But I fancy that you
will not be incredulous. As I watched you and listened to you on
Christmas Day, I thought I saw in you one to whom the supernatural was more than a beautiful and symbolical fairy story, and
one who held it not impossible that this unseen should sometimes
manifest itself. As you reminded us, the Religion of the Incarnation rests on the fact that the Infinite and the Eternal expresses
Himself in terms of space and time; and that it is in this that the
greatness of the Love of God consists. Since then, as you said, the
Creation, the Incarnation, and the Sacramental System alike, in
various degree, are the manifestation of God under these condi-

tions, surely it cannot be 'materialistic' (whatever that exactly means), to believe that the 'spiritual' world and the personages that inhabit it sometimes express themselves in the same manner as their Maker. However, will you have patience with me while I tell you this story? I cannot believe that such a grace should be kept in darkness.

"I was about seven years old when my mother died, and my father left me chiefly to the care of servants. Either I must have been a difficult child, or my nurse must have been a hard woman: but I never gave her my confidence. I had clung to my mother as a saint clings to God: and when I lost her, it nearly broke my heart. Night after night I used to lie awake, with the firelight in the room, remembering how she would look in on her way to bed; when at last I slept it seems to me now as if I never did anything but dream of her; and it was only to wake again to that desolate emptiness. I would torture myself by closing my eyes, and fancying she was there, and then opening them and seeing the room empty. I would turn and toss and sob without a sound. I suppose that I was as near the limit that divides sanity from madness as it is possible to be. During the day I would sit on the stairs when I could get away from my nurse, and pretend that my mother's footsteps were moving overhead, that her door opened, that I heard her dress on the carpet: again I would open my eyes, and in self-cruelty compel myself to understand that she was gone. Then again I would tell myself that it was all right: that she was away for the day, but would come back at night. In the evenings I would be happier, as the time for her return drew nearer; even when I said my prayers I would look forward to the moment, into which I had cheated myself in believing, when the door would open, after I was in bed, and my mother look in. Then as the time passed, my false faith would break down, and I would sob myself to sleep, dream of her, and sob myself awake again. As I look back it appears to me as if this went on for months: I suppose, however, in reality, it could not have been more than a very few weeks, or my reason would have given way. And at last I was caught on the edge of the precipice, and drawn lovingly back to safety and peace.

"I used to sleep alone in the night nursery at this time, and my nurse occupied a room opening out of it. The night nursery had two doors, one at the foot of my bed, and one at the further end of the room, in the corner diagonally opposite to that in which the head of my bed stood. The first opened upon the landing, and the second into my nurse's room, and this latter was generally kept a few inches open There was no light in my room, but a nightlight was kept burning in the nurse's room, so that even without the firelight my room was not in total darkness.

"I was lying awake one night (I suppose it would be about eleven o'clock), having gone through a dreadful hour or two of misery, half-waking and half-sleeping. I had been crying quietly, for fear my nurse should hear through the partly opened door, burying my hot face in the pillow. I was feeling really exhausted, listening to my own heart, and cheating myself into the half-faith that its throbs were the footsteps of my mother coming towards my room; I had raised my face and was staring at the door at the foot of my bed, when it opened suddenly without a sound; and there, as I thought, my mother stood, with the light from the oil lamp outside shining upon her. She was dressed, it seemed, as once before I had seen her in London, when she came into my room to bid me goodnight before she went out to an evening party. Her head shone with jewels that flashed as the firelight rose and sank in the room, a dark cloak shrouded her neck and shoulders, one hand held the edge of the door, and a great jewel gleamed on one of her fingers. She seemed to be looking at me.

"I sat up in bed in a moment, amazed but not frightened, for was it not what I had so often fancied? and I called out to her:

"'Mother, mother!'

"At the word she turned and looked on to the landing, and gave a slight movement with her head, as if to someone waiting there, either of assent or dismissal, and then turned to me again. The door closed silently, and I could see in the firelight, and in the faint glimmer that came through the other door, that she held out her arms to me. I threw off the bedclothes in a moment, and scrambled down to the end of the bed, and she lifted me gently in her arms, but said no word. I too said nothing, but she raised the cloak a little and wrapped it round me, and I lay there in bliss, my head on her shoulder, and my arm round her neck. She walked smoothly and noiselessly to a rocking chair that stood beside the fire and sat down, and then began to rock gently to and fro. Now it may be difficult to believe, but I tell you that I neither said anything, nor desired to say anything. It was enough that she was there. After a little while I suppose I fell asleep, for I found myself in an agony of tears and trembling again, but those arms held me firmly, and I was soon at peace; still she spoke no word, and I did not see her face.

"When I woke again she was gone, and it was morning, and I was in bed, and the nurse was drawing up the blind, and the winter sunshine lay on the wall. That day was the happiest I had known since my mother's death; for I knew she would come again.

"After I was in bed that evening I lay awake waiting, so full of happy content and certainty that I fell asleep. When I awoke the fire was out, and there was no light but a narrow streak that came through the door from my nurse's room. I lay there a minute or two waiting, expecting every moment to see the door open at the foot of my bed; but the minutes passed, and then the clock in the hall below beat three. Then I fell into a passion of tears; the night was nearly gone, and she had not come to me. Then, as I tossed to and fro, trying to stifle my crying, through my tears there came the misty flash of light as the door opened, and there she stood again. Once again I was in her arms, and my face on her shoulder. And again I fell asleep there.

"Now this went on night after night, but not every night, and never unless I awoke and cried. It seemed that if I needed her desperately she came, but only then.

"But there were two curious incidents that occurred in the order in which I will write them down. The second I understand now, at any rate; the first I have never altogether understood, or rather there are several possible explanations.

"One night as I lay in her arms by the fire, a large coal suddenly slipped from the grate and fell with a crash, awaking the nurse in the other room. I suppose she thought something was wrong, for she appeared et the door with a shawl over her shoulders, holding the nightlight in one hand and shading it with the other. I was going to speak, when my mother laid her hand across my mouth. The nurse advanced into the room, passed close beside us, apparently without seeing us, went straight to the empty bed, looked down on the tumbled clothes, and then turned away as if satisfied, and went back to her room. The next day I managed to elicit from her, by questioning, the fact that she had been disturbed in the night, and had come into my room, but had seen me sleeping quietly in bed.

"The other incident was as follows. One night I was lying half-dozing against my mother's breast, my head against her heart, and not, as I usually lay, with my head on her shoulder. As I lay there it seemed to me as if I heard a strange sound like the noise of the sea in a shell, but more melodious. It is difficult to describe it, but it was like the murmuring of a far-off crowd, overlaid with musical pulsations. I nestled closer to her and listened; and then I could distinguish, I thought, innumerable ripples of church bells pealing, as if from another world. Then I listened more intently to the other sound; there were words, but I could not distinguish them. Again and again a voice seemed to rise above the others, but I could hear no intelligible words. The voices cried in every sort of tone — passion, content, despair, monotony. And then as I listened I fell asleep. As I look back now, I have no doubt what voices those were that I heard.

"And now comes the end of the story. My health began to improve so remarkably that those about me noticed it. I never gave way, during the day at any rate, to those old piteous imaginings; and at night, when, I suppose, the will partly relaxes its control, whenever my distress reached a certain point, she was there to comfort me. But her visits grew more and more rare, as I needed her less, and at last ceased. But it is of her last visit, which took place in the spring of the following year, that I wish to speak.

"I had slept well all night, but had awakened in the dark just before the dawn from some dream which I forget but which left my nerves shaken. When in my terror I cried out, again the door opened, and she was there. She stood with the jewels in her hair, and the cloak across her shoulders, and the light from the landing lay partly on her face. I scrambled at once down the bed, and was lifted and carried to the chair, and presently fell asleep. When I awoke the dawn had come, and the birds were stirring and chirping, and a pleasant green light was in the room; and I was still in her arms. It was the first time, except in the instance I have mentioned, that I had awakened except in bed, and it was a great joy to find her there. As I turned a little I saw the cloak which sheltered us both — of a deep blue, with an intricate pattern of flowers and leaves and birds among branches. Then I turned still more to see her face, which was so near me, but it was turned away; and even as I moved she rose and carried me towards the bed. Still holding me on her left arm she lifted and smoothed the bedclothes, and then laid me gently in bed, with my head on the pillow. And then for the first time I saw her face plainly. She bent over me, with one hand on my breast as if to prevent me from rising, and looked straight into my eyes; and it was not my mother.

"There was one moment of blinding shock and sorrow, and I gave a great sob, and would have risen in bed, but her hand held me down, and I seized it with both my own, and still looked in her eyes. It was not my mother, and yet was there ever such a mother's face as that? I seemed to be looking into depths of indescribable tenderness and strength, and I leaned on that strength in those moments of misery. I gave another sob or two as I looked, but I was quieter and at last peace came to me, and I had learned my lesson.

"I did not at the time know who she was, but my little soul dimly saw that my own mother for some reason could not at that time come to me who needed her so sorely, and that another great Mother had taken her place; yet, after the first moment or so, I felt no anger or jealousy, for one who had looked into that kindly face could have no such unworthy thought.

"Then I lifted my head a little, I remember, and kissed the hand that I held in my own, reverently and slowly. I do not know why I did it, except that it was the natural thing to do. The hand was strong and white, and delicately fragrant. Then it was withdrawn, and she was standing by the door, and the door was open; and then she was gone, and the door was closed.

"I have never seen her since, but I have never needed to see her, for I know who she is; and, please God, I shall see her again; and next time I hope my mother and I will be together; and perhaps it will not be very long; and perhaps she will allow me to kiss her hand again.

"Now, my dear sir, I do not know how all this will appear to you; it may seem to you, though I do not think it will, merely childish. Yet, in a sense, I desire nothing more than that, for our Savior Himself told us to be like children, and our Savior too once lay on His Mother's breast. I know that I am getting to be an old man, and that old men are sometimes very foolish; but it more and more seems to me that experience, as well as His words, tells me that the great Kingdom of Heaven has a low and narrow door that only little children can enter, and that we must become little again, and drop all our bundles, if we would go through.

"That, dear and Reverend Sir, is my story. And may I ask you to remember me sometimes at the altar and in your prayers? for surely God will ask much from one to whom He has given so much, and as yet I have nothing to show for it; and my time must be nearly at an end, even if His infinite patience is not.

"Believe me,
"Yours faithfully,
"__ __"

The Bridge over the Stream

"'Lo, I am free! I choose the pain thou bearest
Thou art the messenger of one who waits
Thou wilt reveal the hidden face thou wearest
When my feet falter at the Eternal Gates."

Old Foes.

We were at tea one afternoon on the little low, tiled platform that marked the site of an old summer house. Tall hurdles covered with briar roses on the further side of the path fenced off the rest of the garden from us, and the sun had just sunk below the level of the house, throwing both ourselves and the garden into cool shadow. The servant had brought out the tea things, but he presently returned with something of horror on his face. The old man looked up and saw him.

"What is it, Parker?" he asked.

"There's been an accident, sir. Tom Awcock at the home farm has been drawn into some machine, and they say he must lose both arms, and maybe his life."

The old man turned quite white, and his eyes grew larger and brighter.

"Is the doctor with him?" he asked, in a perfectly steady voice.

"Yes, sir, and they've sent a message, Would you be good enough to step down? The rector's away, and Tom's mother's crying terrible. But not yet, sir. About seven o'clock, they say. It won't be over till then, and there's no immediate danger."

"Tell them I will be there at seven," said the clergyman.

Parker went back to the house, and presently we heard the footsteps of a child running down the drive towards the farm.

"How shocking it is!" I said in a moment or two.

"Ah!" said the old man, smiling, "I have learned my lesson. It is not really so shocking as you think. Does that sound very hard?"

I said nothing, for it seemed to me that all the consolations of religion could not soften the horror of such things. If such agonies are necessary as remedies or atonements, at least they are terrible.

"I learned my lesson," the old man went on, "down the road there outside the hedge — down by the bridge. Would you like to hear it? Or are you tired of an old dreamer's stories?" and he smiled at me.

"Now I know you think that I am hard — that I am a little apart maybe from human life — that I cannot understand the blind misery of those who suffer in ignorance; yet you would be the first, I believe, to think that Mrs. Awcock's consolations are unreal, and that when she tells me that she knows there is a wise purpose behind, she is only repeating what is proper to say to a clergyman. But that is not so; that old threadbare sentence is intensely real to these people, and, I hope, to myself, too. For there is nothing that I desire more than to be a child like them. It is the apparent purposelessness that distresses you: it is the certainty of a deliberate purpose that comforts me. Well, shall I tell you what I saw?"

I was a little distressed at what looked like callousness, but I told him I would like to hear the story.

"I was standing one evening — it would be about five years ago — in the field down there near the stream. You remember the bridge there, over which the road goes, just outside the hedge. I love running water, and I went slowly up and down by the side of the beck. There were children on the road, coming back from school, and they stopped on the bridge to look at the water, as children and old men will. They did not see me, as the field is a little below the road, and besides their backs were turned to me. I could see a pink frock or two, and a pair of stout bare legs. Two girls were taking their brother home — he was between them, a hand clasped by each of the sisters. I suppose the eldest girl would be about nine, and the boy five. They were talking solemnly, and I could hear every word.

"Why are children always supposed to be gay? There is no solemnity in the world to be compared to the solemnity of a little boy, or of his sister who has charge of him.

"One of the girls said, 'Look, Johnny, there are little fishes down there.'

"'When I am a man —' Johnny began, very slowly.

"'Look, Johnny,' said the other girl, 'there's a blue flower.'

"Up to this I remember every word. But then I began to watch Johnny.

"The girls went on talking, but they leaned over more, and I could not hear them plainly. Johnny stealthily withdrew a hand from each of his sisters, and began to look for a stone to throw at the fishes or the blue flower, I suppose; for man is lord of Creation. I could see him presently through the hedge digging patiently with his fingers and loosening a stone that was firm in the road. And at that moment I heard a far away shout and the distant bark of a dog.

"The evening was wonderfully still: every leaf hung quiet: and there were far off clouds heaping themselves up in the west, tower over tower. We had a thunderstorm that night, I remember. The brook was quiet, just slipping noiselessly from pool to pool.

"Still Johnny was digging and the girls were talking. Then out of the village above us came again far off noises. I could hear a rumble and the clatter of hoofs, then a cry or two more, and the nearer terrified yelp of a dog. But the girls were intent on the brook — and Johnny on the stone.

"Even now I did not understand what was happening: but I grew uneasy — and with great difficulty, for I was an old man even then, tried to scramble up the high bank by the bridge. As I reached the top I saw that one of the girls had gone. She had run, I suppose, off the bridge down by the side of the road. The other girl was still standing — but looking in a frightened way up the hill. Down the hill came the loud rumble of a cart and the clatter of hoofs, terribly near.

"The girl by the side of the road began to scream to her sister, who darted off, and then remembered Johnny and turned. Johnny got up too and ran to the parapet and stood against it.

"I was shouting too by now, through the hedge: but I could do nothing more, nothing more, because the hedge was high and thick, and I was an old man. Then in a moment I remembered that shouting would only distract them, and I stopped. It was useless. I could do absolutely nothing. But it was very hard.

"Then I saw the galloping body of a horse through the branches, with a butcher's cart that rocked behind him. There was no one on the cart.

"Now there was room for the cart to pass the boy safely. By the wheel marks, which I looked at afterwards, there were three clear feet — if only the boy had stood still.

"The girls seemed petrified as they stood, one in act to run, the other crouching and hiding her face against the hedge. The cart was now within ten yards, as I could see, though I was still staring at Johnny. Then this is what I saw.

"Somewhere behind him over the parapet of the bridge there was a figure. I remember nothing about it except the face and the hands. The face was, I think, the tenderest I have ever seen. The eyes were downcast, looking upon the boy's head with indescribable love, the lips were smiling. One hand was over the boy's eyes, the other against his shoulder behind. In a moment the memory of other stories I had heard came to mind — and I gave a sob of relief that the boy was safe in such care.

"But as the iron hoofs and rocking wheels came up, the hand on the boy's shoulder suddenly pushed him to meet them; and yet those tender eyes and mouth never flinched, and the child took a step forward in front of the horse, and was beaten down without a cry: and the cart lurched heavily, righted itself, and dashed on out of sight.

"When the cloud of dust had passed, the little body lay quiet on the road, and the two girls were clinging to one another, screaming and sobbing, but there was nothing else.

"I was as angry at first as an old man could be. I nearly (may He forgive me for it now!) cursed God and died. But the memory of that tender face did its work. It was as the face of a mother who nurses her first born child, as the face of a child who kisses a wounded creature, it was as I think the Father's Face itself must have been, which those angels always behold, as He looked down upon the Sacrifice of His only Son.

"Will you forgive me now if I seemed hard a few minutes ago? Perhaps you still think it was hardness that made me speak as I did. But, for myself, I hope I may call it by a better name than that."

In the Convent Chapel

"In her all longings mix and meet;
Dumb souls through her are eloquent
She feels the earth beneath her feet
Vibrate in passionate intent;
Through her our tides of feeling roll,
And find their God within her soul."

The Contemplative Soul

Next evening about this time, on coming indoors for tea, I found the old man seated at the open door that looked on to the lawn, with a book on his knees, and his finger between the pages. He held the book towards me as I came near him, and showed me the title, "The Interior Castle."

"I have just been reading," he said, "Saint Teresa's description of the difference between the intellectual and the imaginative vision. It is curious how she fails really to express it, except to anyone who happens to have had a glimpse already for himself of what she means. I suppose it is one of the signs of reality in the spiritual world that no one can ever describe so much as he knows."

I sat down.

"I am afraid I don't understand a word you are saying," I answered smiling.

For answer he opened the book and read Saint Teresa's curious gasping incoherent sentences — at least so I thought them.

"Still," I said, "I am afraid —"

"Oh," he said almost impatiently, "surely you know now; indeed you know it, but do not recognize it."

"Can you give me any sort of instance?" I asked.

He thought for a moment or two in silence; and then —

"I think I can," he said, "if you are sure it will not bore you."

He poured out tea for us both, and then began:

"Most of the tales I have told you are of the imaginative vision, by which I do not mean that the vision is in any way unreal or untrue, which is what most people mean by 'imaginative,' but only that it presents itself in the form of a visible picture. It seems chiefly the function of the imagination to visualize facts, and it is an abuse of that faculty to employ it chiefly in visualizing fancies. But it is possible for spiritual facts to represent themselves vividly and clearly to the intellect instead. so that the person to whom the intellectual vision is given does not, so to speak, 'see' anything, but only 'apprehends' something to be true. However, this will become more clear presently.

"Some years ago I took my annual holiday in the form of a solitary walking tour. I will not tell you where I went, as there are others concerned in this story who would dislike intensely to be publicly spoken of in the way that I shall have to speak of them; but it is enough to say that I came at last to a little town towards sunset. My object in coming to this place was to visit a convent of enclosed nuns whose reputation for holiness was very great. I carried with me a letter of introduction to the Reverend Mother, which I knew would admit me to the chapel. I left my bag at the inn, and then walked down to the convent, which stood a little way out of the town.

"The lay sister who opened the door to me asked me to come into the parlor while she told the Reverend Mother; and after waiting a few minutes in the prim room with its bees-waxed floor and its religious engravings and objects, a wonderfully dignified little old lady, with a quiet wrinkled face, came in with my letter open in her hand. We talked a few minutes about various things, and I had a glass of cowslip wine in a thick-lipped wineglass.

"She told me that the convent was a very ancient foundation, that it had been country house ever since the Dissolution of the Religious Houses, until about twenty years ago, when it had been acquired for the community. There still remained of the old buildings part of the cloisters, with the south transept of the old church, which was now the chapel; the whole, with a wall or two, forming the courtyard through which I had come. Behind the house lay the garden, on to which the window of the parlor looked; and as I sat I could see a black cross or two marking the nuns' graveyard. I made inquiries as to the way the time of the community was spent.

"'Our object,' said the old lady, 'is perpetual intercession for sinners. We have the great joy of the Blessed Sacrament amongst us in the chapel, and, except during the choir offices and Mass, there is always a nun kneeling before It. We look after one or two ladies incurably ill, who have come to end their days with us, and we make our living by embroidery.'

"I asked how it was that she could receive strangers if the order was an enclosed one.

"'The lay sisters and myself alone can receive strangers. We find that necessary.'

"After a little more talk I asked whether I might see the chapel, and she took me out into the courtyard immediately.

"As we walked across the grass she pointed out to me the cloisters, now built up into a corridor, and the long ruined wall of the old nave which formed one side of the quadrangle. A grave faced and stout collie dog had joined us at the door, and we three went together slowly towards the door in the center of the west wall of the restored transept. The evening sun lay golden on the wall before us and on the ruined base of the central tower of the old church, round which jackdaws wheeled and croaked."

The old priest broke off and turned to me, with his eyes burning:

"What a marvelous thing the Religious Life is," he said, "and above all the Contemplative Life! Here were these nuns as no doubt they and their younger sisters are still, without one single thing that in the world's opinion makes life worth living. There is practically perpetual silence, there are hours to be spent in the chapel, no luxuries, no amusements, no power of choice, they are always rather hungry and rather tired, at the very least. And yet they are not sacrificing; present happiness to future happiness, as the world always supposes, but they are intensely and radiantly happy 'now in this present time.' I don't know what further proof anyone wants of Who our Lord is than that men and women find the keenest, and in fact their only joy, in serving Him and belonging to Him.

"Well, I remember that something of this sort was in my mind as I went across the courtyard beside this motherly old lady with her happy quiet face. She had been over fifty years in Religion, my friend had told me.

"At the door she stopped.

"'I will not come in,' she said, 'but you will find me in the parlor when you come out.'

"And she turned and went back, with the collie walking slowly beside her, his golden plumed tail raised high against her black habit.

"The door was partly open, but a thick curtain hung beyond. I pushed it quietly aside and stepped in. It seemed very dark at first, in contrast to the brilliant sunshine outside; but I presently saw that I was kneeling before a high iron-barred screen, in which was no door. On the left, in the further corner of the chapel, glimmered a blue light in a silver lamp before a statue of our Lady.

"Opposite me rose up the steps before the high altar; but not far away, because, as you remember, the chapel had once been the transept of a church, and the east wall, in the center of which the high altar stood, was longer than both the south wall where a second altar stood, and the modern brick wall that closed it on the north. A slender crucifix in black and white and six thin tapers rose above the altar, and high above stood the Tabernacle closed by a white silk curtain, before which flickered a tiny red spark.

"I said a prayer or two, and then I noticed for the first time a dark outline rising in the center of the space before the altar. For a moment I was perplexed, and then I saw that it was the nun whose hour it was for intercession. Her back was turned to me as she knelt at the faldstool, and her black veil fell in rigid lines on to her shoulders, and mingled with her black serge habit below. There she knelt perfectly motionless, praying. I had not, and have not, a notion as to her age. She might have been twenty-five or seventy.

"As I knelt there I thought deeply, wondering as to the nun's age, how long she had been professed, when she would die, whether she was happy; and, I am afraid, I thought more of her than of Him Who was so near. Then a kind of anger seized me, as I compared in my mind the life of a happy good woman in the world with that of this poor creature. I pictured the life, as one so often sees it in homes, of a mother with her children growing up about her, her hands busy with healthy home work, her life glorified by a good man's love; as she grows older, passing from happy stage to happy stage, comforting, helping, sweetening every soul she meets. Was it not for this that women — and men too, I thought, rebuking myself — were made? Then think of the sour life of the cloister — as loveless and desolate as the cold walls themselves! And even, I thought, even if there is a strange peculiar joy in the Religious Life — even if there is an absence of sorrows and anxieties such as spoil the happiness of many lives in the world — yet, after all, surely the Contemplative Life is useless and barren. The Active Life may be well enough, if the prayers and the discipline issue in greater efficiency, if the priest is more fervent when he ministers outside, and the sister of charity more charitable. Yes, I thought, the active Religious Life is reasonable enough; but the Contemplative —! After all it is essentially selfish, it is a sin against society. Possibly it was necessary when the wickedness of the world was more fierce, to protest against it by this retirement; but not now, not now! How can the lump be leavened if the leaven be withdrawn? How can a soul serve God by forsaking the world which He made and loves?. . ."

"And so," said the priest, turning to me again, "I went on — poor ignorant fool! — thinking that the woman who knelt in front of me was less useful than myself, and that my words and actions and sermons and life did more to advance God's kingdom than her prayers! And then — then — at the moment when I reached that climax of folly and pride, God was good to me and gave me a little light.

"Now, I do not know how to put it — I have never put it into words before, except to myself — but I became aware, in my intellect alone, of one or two clear facts. In order to tell you what those facts were I must use picture language; but remember they are only translations or paraphrases of what I perceived.

"First I became aware suddenly that there ran a vital connection from the Tabernacle to the woman. You may think of it as one of those bands you see in machinery connecting two wheels, so that when either wheel moves the other moves too. Or you may think of it as an electric wire, joining the instrument the telegraph operator uses with the pointer at the other end. At any rate there was this vital band or wire of life.

"Now in the Tabernacle I became aware that there was a mighty stirring and movement. Something within it beat like a vast Heart, and the vibrations of each pulse seemed to quiver through all the ground. Or you may picture it as the movement of a clear deep pool when the basin that contains it is jarred — it seemed like the movement of circular ripples crossing and re-crossing in swift thrills. Or you may think of it as that faint movement of light and shade that may be seen in the heart of a white-hot furnace. Or again you may picture it as sound — as the sound of a high ship mast with the rigging, in a steady wind; or the sound of deep woods in a July noon."

The priest's face was working, and his hands moved nervously.

"How hopeless it is," he said, "to express all this! Remember that all these pictures are not in the least what I perceived. They are only grotesque paraphrases of a spiritual fact that was shown me.

"Now I was aware that there was something of the same activity in the heart of the woman, but I did not know which was the controlling power. I did not know whether the initiative sprang from the Tabernacle and communicated itself to the nun's will; or whether she, by bending herself upon the Tabernacle, set in motion a huge dormant power. It appeared to me possible that the solution lay in the fact that two wills cooperated, each reacting upon the other. This, in a kind of way, appears to me now true as regards the whole mystery of free will and prayer and grace.

"At any rate the union of these two represented itself to me, as I have said, as forming a kind of engine that radiated an immense light or sound or movement. And then I perceived something else too.

"I once fell asleep in one of those fast trains from the north, and did not awake until we had reached the terminus. The last thing I had seen before falling asleep had been the quiet darkening woods and fields through which we were sliding, and it was a shock to awake in the bright humming terminus and to drive through the crowded streets, under the electric glare from the lamps and windows. Now I felt something of that sort now. A moment ago I had fancied myself apart from movement and activity in this quiet convent; but I seemed somehow to have stepped into a center of busy, rushing life. I can scarcely put the sensation more clearly than that. I was aware that the atmosphere was charged with energy; great powers seemed to be astir, and I to be close to the whirling center of it all.

"Or think of it like this. Have you ever had to wait in a City office? If you have done that you will know how intense quiet can coexist with intense activity. There are quiet figures here and there round the room. Or it may be there is only one such figure — a great financier — and he sitting there almost motionless. Yet you know that every movement tingles, as it were, out from that still room all over the world. You can picture to yourself how people leap to obey or to resist — how lives rise and fall, and fortunes are made and lost, at the gentle movements of this lonely quiet man in his office. Well, so it was here. I perceived that this black figure knelt at the center of reality and force, and with the movements of her will and lips controlled spiritual destinies for eternity. There ran out from this peaceful chapel lines of spiritual power that lost themselves in the distance, bewildering in their profusion and terrible in the intensity of their hidden fire. Souls leaped up and renewed the conflict as this tense will strove for them. Souls even at that moment leaving the body struggled from death into spiritual life, and fell panting and saved at the feet of the Redeemer on the other side of death. Others, acquiescent and swooning in sin, woke and snarled at the merciful stab of this poor nun's prayers."

The priest was trembling now with excitement.

"Yes," he said; "yes, and I in my stupid arrogance had thought that my life was more active in God's world than hers. So a small provincial shopkeeper, bustling to and fro behind the counter, might think, if only he were mad enough, that his life was more active and alive than the life of a director who sits at his table in the City. Yes, that is a vulgar simile; but the only one that I can think of which in the least expresses what I knew to be true. There lay my little foolish narrow life behind me, made up of spiritless prayers and efforts and feeble dealings with souls; and how complacent I had been with it all, how self-centered, how out of the real tide of spiritual movement! And meanwhile, for years probably, this nun had toiled behind these walls in the silence of grace, with the hum of the world coming faintly to her ears, and the cries of peoples and nations, and of persons whom the world accounts important, sounding like the voices of children at play in the muddy street outside: and indeed that is all that they are, compared to her — children making mud pies or playing at shop outside the financier's office."

The priest was silent, and his face became quieter again. Then in a moment he spoke again.

"Well," he said, "that is what I believe to have been an intellectual vision. There was no form or appearance or sound; but I can only express what was shown to me to be true, under those images. It almost seems to me as I look back now as if the air in the chapel were full of a murmurous sound and a luminous mist as the currents of need and grace went to and fro. But I know really that the silence was deep and the air dim."

Then I made a foolish remark.

"If you feel like that about the Contemplative Life, I wonder you did not try to enter it yourself."

The priest looked at me for a moment.

"It would be rash, surely, for a little shopkeeper of no particular ability to compete with Rothschild."

Under Which King?

All such knowledge as this, whether it comes from God or not,
can be but of little profit to the soul in the way of perfection, if it
trusts to it: yea, rather, if it is not careful to reject it, . . . it will
bring upon it great evil; . . . for all the dangers and
inconveniences of the supernatural apprehensions, and many
more, are to be found here."

The Ascent of Mount Carmel.

Within a day or two of our conversation on St. Teresa, I
asked the old priest about what is called "Quietism." A
friend had given me an old copy of Molinos' *Spiritual Guide,* and I
knew that the writer had been condemned and imprisoned for life,
and yet I could not understand in what lay his crime.

"It is difficult to put into words," said the priest, "or even to
understand, why certain sentences are condemned, since it is probably possible to parallel them from other Catholic mystics whose
names are honored. Yet the fact remains that the result of Molinos'
teaching was neglect of the Sacraments and of external means of
grace, which was not so in the case of the schools of other mystics."

"But I will tell you a story," he went on, "to illustrate the effect of
certain kinds of mysticism; and I must leave you to judge whether
my friend was right or wrong in what he decided, for I must tell
you first that the incident did not happen to me. On the whole I
may say that I have my own opinion on the subject, but I will not
tell you what it is, as sometimes I am strongly inclined to change it.
However, you shall hear the story. Shall we take a stroll on the terrace?"

And when we had reached it, he began:

"My friend was a priest of about thirty years of age (this happened some forty years ago). He was working in the country at the time, and had a great deal of leisure for reading, and this he chiefly occupied in the study of various mystics, and most of them of the Quietistic school. You know, too, that one of their characteristic lines of thought lies in the abandonment of all effort save that of adhering to God, and even that is to be a passive rather than an active effort. The soul must lie still, says one of them, and be drawn as if by a rope up the Mount of Perfection. The slightest movement will check or divert that swift and steady approach towards God.

"But my friend not only studied writers of this school intellectually, but he put himself more or less under their spiritual direction. He told me afterwards that it seemed to him that if he used the Sacraments faithfully, and if he found that his devotion towards them did not cool, he would be sufficiently protected against possible extravagances or heresies in his spiritual reading. His daily meditation, too, he told me, began to mean more to him than ever in his lifetime: the presence of God seemed more real and accessible, and, above all, the guidance of God in his daily life more apparent. The time that really matters, as he said to me once, is the time between our religious exercises; and in this time, too, God manifested Himself. In fact, from all that he said to me, I have very little doubt that his character and spiritual life were both deepened and purified, at any rate at first, by his devotional study of these mystics.

"One word more before I begin the actual story.

"I said just now that the guidance of God began to be more apparent in his daily life. There are two main ways of settling questions that come up for decision, and both ways are possible to a religious man. One way is to lay stress on the intellectual side, to weigh the arguments carefully, and decide, as it were, by reasoning alone: the other is to lay comparatively little stress on the arguments and the intellectual side generally, and to make the main effort lie in the aspiration of the will towards God for guidance. We may call them, roughly, the intellectual and the intuitive. Now of course my friend's mystical studies inclined him more and more towards the latter. He told me, in fact, that in the most ordinary questions — in his visiting his people — in his preaching — in his dealings with souls — he began more and more to refuse intellectual light, and to trust instead to the immediate interior guidance of the Holy Ghost. More than once, for example, he laid aside the sermon he had prepared, as he entered the pulpit, and preached from a text that had seemed to be suggested to him. Of course it was not so good from the literary point of view; but that, as he very justly said, is not the most important question in judging of a sermon. He seemed to find, he told me, that his spiritual power in every way developed, both in his interior life and in his dealings with others.

"In his conversations, too, he would allow long silences to come, if it did not seem to him that God moved him to speak; at other times he would drop conventional modes of speech and say things that, humanly judged, were calculated to do the very opposite of what he personally desired. Sometimes in such a case his wish was attained, and sometimes not; but in both cases he forced himself to regard it as if he had succeeded. In short, he acted and spoke in obedience to this interior drawing, and disregarded consequences entirely. And this, I need hardly say, is one road to interior peace.

"And then at last a startling thing happened.

"There had been some crime committed: I have not an idea what it was. Two men were involved in the consequences. One, whom we will call A., had committed the crime: but he could only be prosecuted if B., whom he had seriously injured, consented to take action. Now my friend was deeply interested in A., and he thought he knew that the one chance of A's salvation lay in his being allowed to go unpunished. But Lord B., who, by the way, was an Irish peer, of no importance himself, though his father had been well known, was a hard, vindictive man, and had publicly announced his intention of ruining A. In this state of affairs my friend was asked to intercede by A. and his friends.

"Lord B. lived in a large country house some four or five miles from my friend's house. He was an unmarried man, but generally had his house fairly full of his friends, who did not bear the best possible reputation.

"My friend arrived at the house by appointment with B., whom he did not personally know, towards the close of a rainy autumn afternoon. In spite of his anxiety he had resolved to be guided as usual by the interior monitor whom he had learned to trust, and he had hardly thought of a single argument which he could use. Yet he felt confident that he was right in coming, and equally confident that he would know what to say when the time came. As he got near the house this confident sense of guidance increased to an extent that almost terrified him. It seemed to him, as he walked under the dripping yellow branches, that a strong, almost physical, oppression carried him forward. As if in a dream he saw the man-servant appear in answer to his ring, and heard, as from a great distance, the man tell him that Lord B. had come in a little while before, and was now expecting him in the smoking room.

"On entering the house these curious sensations, which he hardly attempted to describe to me, seemed to diminish a little, and he felt cool and confident. He told me that the sense of oppression resting on him was dispelled, as if by a breeze, as he passed along the corridor on the ground floor on his way to the smoking room in the west wing of the house.

"The servant threw open the door and announced him, and my friend went through, and the door closed behind him; but the moment he had crossed the threshold he felt that something was wrong.

"There was a circle of men, some in shooting costume, and some as if they had not been out all day, sitting in easy chairs round the fire, which was to the right of the door. My friend could see most of their faces, and Lord B.'s face among them, as he paused at the door; but not one offered to move, though all looked curiously at him.

"There was silence for a moment, and then Lord B. said suddenly and loudly:

"'Well, here's the parson at last, sermon and all.'

"And then two or three of the men laughed.

"My friend saw of course that Lord B. had arranged the interview in this way simply in order to insult him, and that he would not be able to speak to him in private at all, as he had hoped. There was, he told me, just one great heave of anger in his heart at this offensive behavior; but he did his best to crush it down, and still stood without speaking. He had not, he said, an idea what to say or do, so he stood and waited.

"Lord B. got up in a moment and lit a cigarette with his back to my friend; and then turned and faced him, leaning against the mantelpiece.

"'Well,' he said, 'we're all waiting.'

"Still there was silence. One of the men beyond the fire suddenly laughed.

"'Now then,' said Lord B. impatiently, "for God's sake say what you came to say, and go.'

"As this sentence ended my friend felt a curious sensation run over him, like those he had experienced in the park, but far stronger. He could never give me any description of it, except by saying that it seemed as if a force were laying hold of him in every remote fiber of his bodily and spiritual being. His own will seemed to give up the control into some stronger hand, and he felt a sense of being steadied and quieted.

"Then he was aware that his own voice said a single sentence of some half-dozen words; but though he heard each word, it was instantly obliterated from his mind. In his description of it all to me afterwards, he said it was like words that we hear immediately before we fall asleep in a lecture room or a railway carriage: each word is English and intelligible, but the sentence conveys no impression.

"While his voice spoke for perhaps two or three seconds, his eyes were fixed on Lord B.'s face, and in that momentary interval he saw a terrible fear and astonishment suddenly stamped upon it. The mouth opened in loose lines and the cigarette fell out, and B.'s hands rose instinctively as if to keep my friend off. One of the men, too, at the further end of the circle suddenly sprang erect, with the same kind of imploring horror on his face.

"That was all that my friend had time to see; for the same power that had laid hold of him turned him immediately to the door, and he opened it and went out and down the corridor. As he went the strange sensation passed, but he felt the sweat prick to his skin and then pour down his face. He heard, too, as he reached the end of the corridor, a bell peal violently somewhere. He passed out into the hall, and even as he opened the front door a servant dashed past him through the hall and down the corridor, up which he had just come.

"He went straight home, feeling terribly tired and overwrought, and had to go to bed on reaching his house, tortured by neuralgia.

"Two hours later a note was brought by a groom from Lord B., written in a shaking hand, with an abject apology for his reception in the afternoon; an entreaty to him not to mention the subject again which he had spoken of in the sitting room, with a scarcely veiled offer of a bribe, and an emphatic promise to withdraw all proceedings against A.

"On the following day he was told that Lord B. was supposed to be unwell, and that the house party had been hurriedly broken up the night before.

"From that day to this he has never had an idea of what the sentence was that his voice spoke that worked such a miracle."

"That is a most curious story," I said. "What do you make of it?"

The priest smiled.

"I will tell you what my friend made of it. He gave up his study of mysticism, yet without in any sense condemning that line of thought of which I have spoken. His reasons, which he explained to me after coming to a decision, were that such a visitation might or might not be from God. If it were not from God, then that proved that he had been meddling with high things, and had somehow slipped under some other control. If it were from God, it might be that it was just for that very purpose that he had been brought so far, but that he dared not pursue that path without some distinct further sign. 'In any case,' he said, 'no soul can be lost by following the simple and well-beaten path of ordinary devotion and prayer.' And so he returned to intellectual forms of meditation, such as most Christians use. He died a few years ago, full of holiness and good works.

"But for you there are several opinions open. Either that it was an intensely strong case of hypnotic thought-transference from Lord B. to my friend, and that the latter only spoke mechanically of something that lay in the former's mind; or you may decide that the whole affair was of the Evil One, and that A. would have been all the better for prosecution, and that an evil being somehow found entrance into the strained nature of my friend, and used it for his own purposes; or that the prophetic gift was bestowed on him but that the ordeal was too fierce and he too cowardly to claim it., And there are other solutions as well, no doubt possible.

"For myself I think I have formed my opinion; but I would prefer, as Herodotus says, to keep it to myself."

With Dyed Garments

"Jesu, well ought I love Thee,
For Thou me showest Thy rood-tree,
Thy crown of thorns, and nails three
The sharp spear that pierced Thee."

Swete Jhesu now wil I

When the second post came in one morning I saw a letter addressed to the priest, in the trembling large characters of an old man's hand, lying upon the slab in the hall. When I came in to lunch I found the old clergyman with an open letter in his hand, and his face full of almost childish happiness.

"I have heard from my oldest friend," he said, making a little movement with the letter. "It is months since he has written. I have known him ever since we were boys."

We sat down to lunch, but he kept on referring to his friend, and to the pleasure the letter gave him.

"We are always planning to meet," he said to me presently. "But we never can manage it. We are both so old. He is much more active than I am, however. He is full of good works, while I, as you know, lead an idle life. I could not take charge of a church. It is all I can do now to serve my own little chapel upstairs."

"Where is he working?" I asked.

"'I think perhaps you fancy he is in Holy Orders, but he is not. He has been on the Stock Exchange till a few years ago, and now he is living in the country, getting ready to die, as he tells me. But he is full of good works; his letter here has news about the village, and of a man whose acquaintance he has made in the reading room there, which he himself built a year ago; but he is full of plans too, and asks my advice."

"It is not often you come across a business man like that," I said.

"No, he is wonderful, but he has been like that for years. He has done a great deal all his life among poor people in London. For years he never missed his two or three nights a week in some club, or on some committee, or visiting sick people."

I began to think that it might have been through the friendship of the priest that this man had been such a worker. But presently he began again.

"Perhaps the most wonderful thing was the way he first began to do such work. Let me see, have I mentioned his name? No? Then I can tell you, otherwise it would not be discreet; that is —" he added, "if you would care to hear."

I told him I should be very much interested.

"Then after lunch we will have coffee in the garden, and I will tell you."

When we had sat down under the shade of a wall, with the tall avenue of pines opposite us making a dark tangled frieze against the delicate sky, he began.

"What I am going to tell you now has been gathered partly from conversations with my friend, and partly from letters he has written to me. Years ago I jotted down the order of events, with names and dates, but that, of course, I fear I cannot show even to you. However, I know the story well, and you may rely on the main facts.

"I must tell you first that many years ago now, my friend, who was about forty years old, had lately become a partner in his father's firm: and of course was greatly occupied with all the details of business. It was a broker's firm, well established and did a good steady business. My friend at that time had no idea of doing any work outside his occupation. I heard him say in fact, about this time, that his work seemed to absorb all his energies and capacity. Then the first event of the series took place.

"He was coming home one frosty afternoon in December, between three and four o'clock, on the top of an omnibus. He was sitting in front and looking about him. He noticed a poorly dressed man standing on the pavement on the right-hand side, as if he wished to cross. Then he began to cross, and came at last right up to the omnibus on which my friend was sitting, and paused a moment to let it pass. As he stood there, my friend watching him with that listless interest with which a tired man will observe details, a hansom cab moving quickly came in the opposite direction. It seemed as if the horse would run the man down. It was too sudden to warn him, but the man saw it, and to avoid the horse sprang quickly forward, his head half turned away, and his feet came between the front and back wheels of the omnibus. There was a jolt and a terrible scream, and my friend horrified leaned far over the side to see. When the omnibus had passed, the man stood for a moment on his crushed feet, and then swayed forward and fell on his face. My friend started up and made a movement to go to him, but several others had seen the accident and ran to the man, and a policeman was crossing quickly from the other side, so he sat down again and the omnibus carried him on.

"Now this horrible thing remained in my friend's mind, haunted him, shocked him profoundly. He could not forget the terrible face of pain that he had seen upturned for an instant, and his imagination carried him on in spite of himself to dwell on the details of those crushed feet. He wrote me a long letter a week or two afterwards, minutely describing all that I have told you.

"The following summer he was going down to the Kennington Oval one Saturday afternoon to see the close of some famous cricket match. He traveled by the Underground Railway as far as Westminster, and from there determined to walk at least across the Bridge. He walked on the right hand side, and had reached the steps of St. Thomas' Hospital. He waited here a moment undecided whether to walk on or drive.

"As he waited, he half turned and saw a beggar sitting in the angle between the steps and the wall. There was a white dog beside him. The beggar's face was partly bandaged; but what caught my friend's attention most were his two hands. They were lying palms downwards on the beggar's knees, bandaged like his face, but in the center of each was a dark spot, showing through the wrapping, as if there were a festering wound that soaked through from underneath. My friend looked at him in disgust for a moment: but terribly fascinated by those quiet suffering hands; and then he passed on. But during all that afternoon he could not forget those hands. I daresay he was overwrought and nervous. But his memory too went back to the accident by the Marble Arch. That night too, as he told me in a conversation afterwards, as he tossed about, his windows wide open to catch the night air, half waking visions kept moving before him of a man with crushed feet and bandaged hands, who moaned and lifted a drawn face to the sky.

"Early that autumn he was alone, except for the servants, in his father's house in London. A maid was taken ill. I forget the nature of the illness, but perhaps you will be able to identify it when I have finished. At any rate the girl grew quickly worse. One morning just before he started to the City the doctor, who had called early that morning, asked to have a word with him, and told him he thought he ought to operate immediately, and asked for his sanction.

"'Well,' said my friend, 'of course I must speak to the girl about it. Have you told her yet?'

"'No,' said the doctor, 'I thought I should mention it to you first. I understand that the girl has no relations in the world.'

"'Can you tell me the nature of the operation?' asked my friend.

"'It is not really serious. It is an incision in the right side,' and he added a few details explaining the case.

"'Well,' said my friend, 'we had better go upstairs together.'

"They went up and found the girl perfectly conscious and reasonable. She consented to the operation, which was fixed for that evening.

"But all that day the picture floated before his eyes of the quiet room at the top of the house, and the girl lying there waiting. And then the scene would shift a little. And he would see the girl after it was over, with a bandage against her side, and the knowledge of the little wound beneath. When he reached home, late in the evening, the doctor was waiting for him.

"'It has been perfectly successful,' he said, 'and I think she will recover.'

"Now, that evening, as my friend sat at the dinner table alone, smoking and thinking, his old experiences came to his mind again. In less than a year he had seen three things, none of which seemed to have any very close relation to him, but each of which had deeply affected him. He told me afterwards that he began to suspect a design underlying them; but he had not a glimmer of light, strange as it may seem to you and me, as to the nature of that design. Within a month, however, I received a letter from him, from some place in the country where he was staying, describing the following incident.

"He had gone down from a Saturday to Monday to a friend's house in Surrey. On the Sunday afternoon he and his friend went for a walk through some woods. Autumn was in full glory, and the trees were blazing in red and gold: and the bramble branches were weighed down with purple fruit. As they walked together along a grass ride they heard shouts and laughter of children in the woods on one side. They could hear footsteps pattering through dry leaves, and the tearing and trampling of brushwood; and in a moment more a boy burst out of the thin hedge, tripped in a bramble, and rolled into the grass walk. He was up again in a moment laughing and flushed, but my friend saw across his forehead a little thin red dotted line where a thorn had scratched him. As the boy laughed up into their faces, he lifted his hand to his forehead.

"'Why it's wet,' he said, and then, looking at his fingers: 'Why, it's blood! I've scratched myself.'

"Other footsteps came running through the undergrowth, and the boy himself ran off down the road, and the footsteps in the wood stopped, retraced themselves and died away in faint rustlings up the hill. But as my friend had looked he had seen in his memory those other experiences of the last year. And all seemed to concentrate themselves on one Figure — with wounded feet and hands and side — and a torn forehead.

"My friend stood quiet so long that his companion spoke to him and touched his arm.

"'Yes, I am ready,' he said; 'let us go home.'

"The end of the letter I cannot quote to you. It is too intimate and personal. But it ended with a request to myself to give him an introduction to some friend who would give him work to do in some poor district. And work of that kind he has carried on ever since."

The old priest's voice ceased.

"There is one thing my friend did not know," he said after a moment. "When that particular operation on the side is performed, of which I have spoken, there comes out blood and water. A doctor will tell you so."

And then:

"That is my friend's story," he said.

"Do you not think it remarkable?"

Unto Babes

"Saint Bernard speaks of the words of Job that he says: '*Abscondit lucem in manibus*'(that is to say, 'God has light hid in His hands'); — 'Thou wot well, he that has a candle a-light between his hands, he may hide it and show it at his own will. So does our Lord to His chosen.'"

The Abbey of the Holy Ghost

A few days after the conversation I have described my visit to the old man came to an end, and my work drew me back to London; but I left behind me a promise to return and spend Christmas at his house. He in the meantime would, he promised me, try to put together some other stories for me against the time that I should return. There were many others, he said, that he had come across in his life which he hoped would interest me, besides a few more personal experiences of his own.

And so I left him smiling and waving to me from his bedroom window that overlooked the drive (for I had to go by an early train), with the clean-shaven face of his old servant looking at me discreetly and gravely from the clear-glass chapel window next to the priest s room, where he had been setting things ready before his master was dressed.

It was a dark winter afternoon when I returned, a week or so before Christmas.

The coachman told me on my inquiry that his master seemed very much aged during the autumn and winter, that he had scarcely left the house since the leaves had fallen, except to sit for an hour or two in sunshiny weather in the sheltered angle of the wall where was the tiled platform that I have spoken of; and that he was afraid he had been suffering from depression. There had been days of almost complete silence, at least so Parker had told him, when the master had sat all day turning over letters and books and old drawers.

I reproached myself with having troubled the old man with demands for more stories; and feared that it had been in the attempt to please me that he had fallen brooding over the past, perhaps dwelling too much on sorrows of which I knew nothing.

As we passed under the pines that tossed their somber plumes in the wind, the sun, breaking through clouds in an angry glory on my right, blazed on the little square-paned windows of the house on my left. The chapel window on the top story seemed especially full of red light streaming from within, but the flame swept across the upper story as we drove past, and left the windows blank and colorless just before we turned the corner at the back of the house.

The old man met me in the hall, and I was startled to see the change that had come to him. His eyes seemed larger than ever, and there was a sorrow in them that I had not seen before. They had been the eyes of a stainless child, wide and smiling; now they were the eyes of one who was under some burden almost too heavy to be borne. In the stronger light of the sitting room as the candles shone on his face, I saw that my impression had only been caused by a drooping of the eyelids, that now hung down a little further. But it looked a tired face.

He welcomed me, and said several charming things to me that I should be ashamed to quote, but he made me feel that he was glad that I had come; and so I was glad too. But he said among other things this:

"I am glad you have come now, because I think I shall have something further to tell you. I have had indications during this autumn that the end is coming, and I think that if I have to pass through a dark valley, — and I feel that I am at its entrance even now, — I think that He will give me His staff as well as His rod. But I am an old man and full of fancies, so please do not question me. But I am very glad," and he took my hand and stroked it for a moment, "very glad that you are here, because I do not think that you will be afraid."

During the following days he told me many stories, bringing out the old books and letters of which the coachman had spoken, and spelling out notes through his tortoiseshell glass, as he sat by the open fireplace in the central sitting room, with the logs crackling and overrun with swift sparks as they rested on their bed of ashes. The door into the garden where the old drive had once been was now kept closed, and a heavy curtain hung over it.

We did not go out very much together — only in the early afternoons we would walk for an hour or so, he leaning on my arm and on a stick, up and down the terraced walk that lay next the drive under the pines, as the sunset burned across the hills like a far-away judgment. Some day perhaps I will write out some of the stories that he told me, although not all. I have the notes by me.

Here is one of them.

We were walking on one of these dark winter afternoons very slowly uphill towards the village that the priest might get a change from the garden. The morning had been gusty and wet, with sleet showers and even a sprinkle of pure snow as the sky cleared after lunch-time; and now the weather was settling down for a frost, and the snow lay thinly here and there on the rapidly hardening ground.

"It is remarkable," the old man was saying to me, "how in spite of our Lord's words people still think that faith is a matter more or less of intellect. Such a phrase as 'intelligent faith' is, of course, strictly most incorrect."

He stopped and looked at me as he said this, as if prepared for dispute. I did not disappoint him.

"You are very puzzling;" I said. "I cannot believe that you do not value intellect. Surely it is a gift of God, and therefore may adorn faith, as any other gift may do."

"Yes," he said, walking on, "it may adorn it; but it has nothing more to do with it really than jewels have to do with a beautiful woman. In fact, sometimes faith is far more beautiful unadorned, and it is quite possible to crush a delicate and growing faith with a weight of learned arguments intended to adorn and perfect it. Christian apologetics, it seems to me, are only really useful in the mouth of one who realizes their entire inadequacy. You can demonstrate nothing of God. You can, by arguments, draw a number of lines that converge towards God, and render His existence and His attributes probable; but you cannot reach Him along those lines. Faith depends not on intellectual but on moral conditions. 'Blessed are the pure in heart,' said our Savior, not 'Blessed are the profound or acute of intellect' — 'for they shall see God.' It is certainly true of intellectual as of all other riches that they who possess them shall find difficulty in entering into the kingdom of God."

"And so," I said, "you think that intellectual powers are not things to covet, and that education is not a very important question after all?"

"No more than wealth," he answered, "at least so far as you mean by education instruction in demonstrable facts or exact sciences. The point of our existence here is to know God. Well, you know for yourself how the race for wealth is ruining millions of souls today. No less surely is keen intellectual competition ruining souls. Mr. —, for instance," he said, naming a well-known critic and poet; "was there ever a man of keener and finer intellect, or of more unerring instinct in matters of literary taste? Well, once I talked with that man most of a day on all his own subjects; in fact, he did nearly all the talking, and I was astonished, I must confess, at the perfection of the training of his already brilliant powers. So much I could perceive, though of course I could not follow him. And of course there were many delicate shades of beauty, if not much more, invisible to me in his talk and criticism. His scale of intellectual beauty ran up out of my sight altogether. But what astonished me more was the coarseness and dullness of his spiritual instinct. I will not call him a child in matters of faith, because that would be high praise; but he was just an ill-bred boor. I have known many a Sussex villager of far purer and finer spiritual fiber. No, no; faith can and does exist quite apart from intellect; and to increase or develop the one often means the decrease and incoherence of the other. *Seigneur, donnez-moi la foi du charbonnier*"

I must confess that this was a new point of view for me; and I am not sure now whether I do not still think it exaggerated and dangerous; but I said nothing, because it did seem to open up difficult questions, and also to throw light on other difficult questions. The priest turned to me again as he walked.

"Why, it must be so," he said; "if it were not, clever people would have a better hope of salvation than stupid people; and that is absurd — as absurd as if rich people should be nearer God than poor people. No, no; talents are distributed unevenly, it is true: to one ten and to another five; but each has one pound, all alike."

We had reached the top of the slope, and the towering hedges had gradually fallen away, so that we could now see far and wide over the country. Away behind us, as we paused for breath, we could see the misty Brighton downs, while in the middle distance lay tumbled wooded hills, with smoke beginning to curl up here and there from the evening fires of hidden villages. The sky was clear overhead, but in the west, where the sunset was beginning to smolder, a few heavy clouds still lingered.

"And God sees all," said the priest.

"Can you put up with another story as we walk home again? I think I ought to be turning now."

We turned and began to retrace our steps downhill.

"This is not an experience of my own," he said. "It was told me by a friend of mine in Cornwall. He was the squire of a little village a few miles out of Truro, and lived there most of the year except a few weeks in the spring, when he would go abroad. He was a man of great learning and taste, but had the faith of a little child. It was like a spring of clear water to hear him speak of God and heavenly things.

"There was a boy in the village who was an idiot. His parents were dead, and he lived alone with his old grandmother, who was a strict Calvinist, and who regarded her grandson as hopelessly damned because his faith and his expression of it were not as hers. There were evident signs, she said, that God's inscrutable decrees were against him. The local preachers there would have nothing to do with the boy; and the clergyman of the parish, after an attempt or two, had given the child up as hopeless. I think my friend told me that the clergyman had tried to teach him Old Testament history.

"Well, the boy was a terrible and disgusting case. I will not go into details beyond saying that the boy's head had the look of a mule about it; his mother, I think, had had a fright shortly before his birth, and the boy used to think sometimes that he was a horse or mule, and the village children used to encourage him in it, and ride and drive him on the green, for he was quite harmless. And so he grew up, neglected and untaught, spending much of his time out of doors, and creeping home on all fours in the evening, snorting and stamping and neighing when he was much excited; and he would stable himself in a corner of the wide dark kitchen, and munch grass; while his grandmother sat in her high chair by the fire reading in her Bible, or looking over her spectacles at the poor misshapen body in the corner that held a damned soul.

"Now my friend hated to see this child. It was the one thing that troubled his faith. Those who have the faith of children have also the troubles of children; and this living example before his eyes of what looked like the carelessness of God, or worse, was a greater offense to my friend's faith than all infidel arguments, or the mere knowledge that such things happened.

"On a certain Christmas Eve my friend had been a long tramp over the hills with a guest who was staying with him for the shooting. They were returning through his own property towards evening, and were just dropping down from the hill. Their path lay along the upper edge of an old disused stone quarry, whose entrance lay perhaps a hundred yards away from the valley road that led into the village — so it was a lonely and unfrequented place. The evening was closing in; and my friend, as he led the way along the path, was trying to make out the outlines of stones and bushes on the floor of the quarry, which lay perhaps seventy feet below them. All at once his eye was caught by the steady glimmer of light somewhere in the dimness beneath, and the sound of a voice. He guessed at once that there were tramps below, and was angry at the thought that they must have willfully disregarded the notice he had put up about making a fire so close to the wood: and he determined to turn them out, and, if need be, to give them shelter for the night in one of his own outhouses. So he stopped and explained

to his friend which path would take him home, while that he himself intended to make his way along the lip of the quarry to the
entrance, and then to go on into its interior where the tramps had
made their camp; and he promised to be at the house five minutes
after his friend.

"So they separated, and he himself soon found his way down a
narrow overgrown path that brought him to the opening of the
quarry.

"It was a good dead darker here, as the hill shadowed it from the
west, and high trees rose on one side; but he was able to stumble
along the stony path which led to the interior, though it grew darker
still as he went. Presently he turned the corner of a tall boulder,
and emerged into the kind of semi-circus that formed the heart of
the quarry: before him, about a third way up the slope, burned the
glimmer of light he had noticed from above, but even as he saw it,
it went out; my friend stood in the path and called out, explaining
who he was, not threatening at all, but offering, if it was anyone
who wanted shelter, to provide it for the night. There was no answer, only the sound of scuffling in the dimness in front, and then
the confused sound of footsteps scrambling; my friend ran forward, calling, and made out presently an oddly shaped thing scrambling over the silt and stone towards a shoulder of rock that stood
out against the sky on his left (I think he said). He tried to follow,
but it was too dark, and after he had stumbled once or twice, he
gave up the pursuit. In a moment more the climbing figure stood
out clear against the sky for an instant, and then disappeared: and
the squire saw with a shock of disgust the mule-like head and
tangled hair rising from the high shoulders of the village idiot, and
his hands dangling on each side of him; and he heard a
high-screaming neighing. But at least, he thought to himself, he
would go and see what the boy had been doing.

"He made his way up the slope of silted gravel and mud that lay
against the face of the rock, and at last reached a little platform
apparently stamped and cut out at the top of the scree just where it
touched the quarry-side. It was too dark for him to distinguish
anything clearly, so he struck a match and held it in the still shel-

tered air while he looked about him. This is what he saw.

"There was a short halter, with a kind of rude head-stall, fastened to a rusty iron staple driven into the rock. There was a little pile of cut grass below it. There was a kind of mud trough constructed against the stone, with a little straw sprinkled in it and holly berries and leaves in front of it; but this showed signs of having been hastily trampled down, though parts of it survived; there were marks of hobnailed boots in it here and there. So much my friend had noticed when the match burned his fingers; but just before he dropped it he noticed something else which made him open his box and light another match; and then he saw the end of a farthing taper sticking out of the ground into which it had been pushed, and another crushed into a ball. He drew out the first and lighted it, and then noticed this last thing. Quite plainly marked on the soft edge of the mud trough, in a place which the hobnailed boots had not touched, was the mark of a tiny child's naked foot, as if a baby had stood in the trough or manger, with one foot on the floor and another on the edge.

"Now I do not know what you think of this, but I know what my friend thought of it, and what I myself think of it. But before he went home he went first to the cottage where the boy lived and found him as usual tethered in the corner, with his grandmother nodding before the fire. The boy would do nothing but snort and stamp: and the grandmother could only say that ten minutes ago the boy had run in and gone straight to his corner as usual. The squire asked whether the boy had been trusted with a child by anyone; but the grandmother said it was impossible. Nor indeed did he ever after hear a word of a child having been missed on that afternoon.

"Then, before he went home, he went to the little church, already decorated for the festival, and there with the fragrance of the holly and yew in the air about him, and the glimmer of a candle near the altar where the church-cleaner was sweeping, he praised the Holy Child whose Birth-night it was, and who had not disdained to lie in a manger and be adored by the beasts of the stall.

"The following morning on his way back from church he went to the quarry again with his friend to show him what he had seen;

but the manger and the holly berries and crumpled taper were all gone, and there was nothing to see but the iron staple and the platform beaten hard and flat."

We had reached the avenue of pines by now that led to the house, and turned in by the little garden gate.

"The story seems to show," the priest added, "that intellect has not much to do with the knowledge of God; and that the things which He hides from the wise and prudent He reveals to babes."

The Traveler

"I am amazed, not that the Traveler returns from that Bourne,
but that he returns so seldom."

The Pilgrims' Way.

O n one of these evenings as we sat together after dinner in
front of the wide open fireplace in the central room of
the house, we began to talk on that old subject — the relation of
Science to Faith.

"It is no wonder," said the priest, "if their conclusions appear
to differ, to shallow minds who think that the last words are being said on both sides; because their standpoints are so different.
The scientific view is that you are not justified in committing
yourself one inch ahead of your intellectual evidence: the religious view is that in order to find out anything worth knowing
your faith must always be a little in advance of your evidence;
you must advance *en échelon* There is the principle of our Lord's
promises. 'Act as if it were true, and light will be given.' The sci-
entist on the other hand says, 'Do not presume to commit yourself until light is given.' The difference between the methods lies,
of course, in the fact that Religion admits the heart and the whole
man to the witness box, while Science only admits the head —
scarcely even the senses. Yet surely the evidence of experience is
on the side of Religion. Every really great achievement is inspired
by motives of the heart, and not of the head; by feeling and passion, not by a calculation of probabilities. And so are the mysteries of God unveiled by those who carry them first by assault; 'The
Kingdom of Heaven suffereth violence; and the violent take it by
force.'

"For example," he continued after a moment, "the scientific view
of haunted houses is that there is no evidence for them beyond
that which may be accounted for by telepathy, a kind of

thought-reading. Yet if you can penetrate that veneer of scientific thought that is so common now, you find that by far the larger part of mankind still believes in them. Practically not one of us really accepts the scientific view as an adequate one."

"Have you ever had an experience of that kind yourself?" I asked.

"Well," said the priest, smiling, "you are sure you will not laugh at it? There is nothing commoner than to think such things a subject for humor; and that I cannot bear. Each such story is sacred to one person at the very least, and therefore should be to all reverent people."

I assured him that I would not treat his story with disrespect.

"Well," he answered, "I do not think you will, and I will tell you. It only happened a very few years ago. This was how it began.

"A friend of mine was, and is still, in charge of a church in Kent, which I will not name; but it is within twenty miles of Canterbury. The district fell into Catholic hands a good many years ago. I received a telegram, in this house, a day or two before Christmas, from my friend, saying that he had been suddenly seized with a very bad attack of influenza, which was devastating Kent at that time; and asking me to come down, if possible at once, and take his place over Christmas. I had only lately given up active work, owing to growing infirmity, but it was impossible to resist this appeal; so Parker packed my things and we went together by the next train.

"I found my friend really ill, and quite incapable of doing anything; so I assured him that I could manage perfectly, and that he need not be anxious.

"On the next day, a Wednesday, and Christmas Eve, I went down to the little church to hear confessions. It was a beautiful old church, though tiny, and full of interesting things: the old altar had been set up again; there was a rood-loft with a staircase leading on to it; and an awmbry on the north of the sanctuary had been fitted up as a receptacle for the Most Holy Sacrament, instead of the old hanging pyx. One of the most interesting discoveries made in the church was that of the old confessional. In the lower half of the rood-screen, on the south side, a square hole had been found, filled up with an insertion of oak; but an antiquarian of the Alcuin Club, whom my friend had asked to examine the church, declared that this without doubt was the place where in the pre-Reformation times confessions were heard. So it had been restored, and put to its ancient use; and now on this Christmas Eve I sat within the chancel in the dim fragrant light, while penitents came and knelt outside the screen on the single step, and made their confessions through the old opening.

"I know this is a great platitude, but I never can look at a piece of old furniture without a curious thrill at a thing that has been so much saturated with human emotion; but, above all that I have ever seen, I think that this old confessional moved me. Through that little opening had come so many thousands of sins, great and little, weighted with sorrow; and back again, in Divine exchange for those burdens, had returned the balm of the Savior's blood. 'Behold! A door opened in heaven,' through which that strange commerce of sin and grace may be carried on — grace pressed down and running over, given into the bosom in exchange for sin! *O bonum commercium!*

The priest was silent for a moment, his eyes glowing. Then he went on.

"Well, Christmas Day and the three following festivals passed away very happily. On the Sunday night after service, as I came out of the vestry, I saw a child waiting. She told me, when I asked her if she wanted me, that her father and others of her family wished to make their confessions on the following evening about six o'clock. They had had influenza in the house, and had not been able to come out before; but the father was going to work next day, as he was so much better, and would come, if it pleased me, and some of his children to make their confessions in the evening and their communions the following morning.

"Monday dawned, and I offered the Holy Sacrifice as usual, and spent the morning chiefly with my friend, who was now able to sit up and talk a good deal, though he was not yet allowed to leave his bed.

"In the afternoon I went for a walk.

"All the morning there had rested a depression on my soul such as I have not often felt; it was of a peculiar quality. Every soul that tries, however poorly, to serve God, knows by experience those heavinesses by which our Lord tests and confirms His own: but it was not like that. An element of terror mingled with it, as of impending evil.

"As I started for my walk along the high road this depression deepened. There seemed no physical reason for it that I could perceive. I was well myself, and the weather was fair; yet air and exercise did not affect it. I turned at last, about half-past three o'clock, at a milestone that marked sixteen miles to Canterbury.

"I rested there for a moment, looking to the south-east, and saw that far on the horizon heavy clouds were gathering; and then I started homewards. As I went I heard a far-away boom, as of distant guns, and I thought at first that there was some sea-fort to the south where artillery practice was being held; but presently I noticed that it was too irregular and prolonged for the report of a gun; and then it was with a sense of relief that I came to the conclusion it was a far-away thunderstorm, for I felt that the state of the atmosphere might explain away this depression that so troubled me. The thunder seemed to come nearer, pealed more loudly three or four times and ceased.

"But I felt no relief. When I reached home a little after four Parker brought me in some tea, and I fell asleep afterwards in a chair before the fire. I was wakened after a troubled and unhappy dream by Parker bringing in my coat and telling me it was time to keep my appointment at the church. I could not remember what my dream was, but it was sinister and suggestive of evil, and, with the shreds of it still clinging to me, I looked at Parker with something of fear as he stood silently by my chair holding the coat.

"The church stood only a few steps away, for the garden and churchyard adjoined one another. As I went down carrying the lantern that Parker had lighted for me, I remember hearing far away to the south, beyond the village, the beat of a horse's hoofs. The horse seemed to be in a gallop, but presently the noise died away behind a ridge.

"When I entered the church I found that the sacristan had lighted a candle or two as I had asked him, and I could just make out the kneeling figures of three or four people in the north aisle.

"When I was ready I took my seat in the chair set beyond the screen, at the place I have described; and then, one by one, the laborer and his children came up and made their confessions. I remember feeling again, as on Christmas Eve, the strange charm of this old place of penitence, so redolent of God and man, each in his tenderest character of Savior and penitent; with the red light burning like a luminous flower in the dark before me, to remind me how God was indeed tabernacling with men, and was their God.

"Now I do not know how long I had been there, when again I heard the beat of a horse's hoofs, but this time in the village just below the churchyard; then again there fell a sudden silence. Then presently a gust of wind flung the door wide, and the candles began to gutter and flare in the draft. One of the girls went and closed the door.

"Presently the boy who was kneeling by me at that time finished his confession, received absolution and went down the church, and I waited for the next, not knowing how many there were.

"After waiting a minute or two I turned in my seat, and was about to get up, thinking there was no one else, when a voice whispered sharply through the hole a single sentence. I could not catch the words, but I supposed they were the usual formula for asking a blessing, so I gave the blessing and waited, a little astonished at not having heard the penitent come up.

"Then the voice began again."

The priest stopped a moment and looked round, and I could see that he was trembling a little

"Would you rather not go on?" I said. "I think it disturbs you to tell me."

"No, no," he said; "it is all right, but it was very dreadful — very dreadful.

"Well, the voice began again in a loud quick whisper, but the odd thing was that I could hardly understand a word; there were just phrases here and there, like the name of God and of our Lady, that I could catch. Then there were a few old French words that I knew; 'le roy' came over and over again. Just at first I thought it must be some extreme form of dialect unknown to me; then I thought it must be a very old man who was deaf, because when I tried, after a few sentences, to explain that I could not understand, the penitent paid no attention, but whispered on quickly without a pause. Presently I could perceive that he was in a terrible state of mind; the voice broke and sobbed, and then almost cried out, but still in this loud whisper; then on the other side of the screen I could hear fingers working and moving uneasily, as if entreating admittance at some barred door. Then at last there was silence for a moment, and then plainly some closing formula was repeated, which gradually grew lower and ceased. Then, as I rose, meaning to come round and explain that I had not been able to hear, a loud moan or two came from the penitent. I stood up quickly and looked through the upper part of the screen, and there was no one there.

"I can give you no idea of what a shock that was to me. I stood there glaring, I suppose, through the screen down at the empty step for a moment or two, and perhaps I said something aloud, for I heard a voice from the end of the church.

"'Did you call, sir?' And there stood the sacristan, with his keys and lantern, ready to lock up.

"I still stood without answering for a moment, and then I spoke; my voice sounded oddly in my ears.

"'Is there anyone else, Williams? Are they all gone?' or something like that.

"Williams lifted his lantern and looked round the dusky church.

"' No, sir; there is no one.'

"I crossed the chancel to go to the vestry, but as I was halfway, suddenly again in the quiet village there broke out the desperate gallop of a horse.

"'There! There!' I cried, 'do you hear that?'

"Williams came up the church towards me.

"'Are you ill, sir?' he said. 'Shall I fetch your servant?'

"I made an effort and told him it was nothing; but he insisted on seeing me home: I did not like to ask him whether he had heard the gallop of the horse; for, after all, I thought, perhaps there was no connection between that and the voice that whispered.

"I felt very much shaken and disturbed; and after dinner, which I took alone of course, I thought I would go to bed very soon. On my way up, however, I looked into my friend's room for a few minutes. He seemed very bright and eager to talk, and I stayed very much longer than I had intended. I said nothing of what had happened in the church; but listened to him while he talked about the village and the neighborhood. Finally, as I was on the point of bidding him goodnight, he said something like this:

"'Well, I mustn't keep you, but I've been thinking while you've been in church of an old story that is told by antiquarians about this place. They say that one of St. Thomas à Becket's murderers came here on the very evening of the murder. It is his day, today, you know, and that is what put me in mind of it, I suppose.'

"While my friend said this, my old heart began to beat furiously; but, with a strong effort of self-control, I told him I should like to hear the story.

"'Oh! There's nothing much to tell,' said my friend; 'and they don't know who it's supposed to have been; but it is said to have been either one of the four knights, or one of the men-at-arms.'

"'But how did he come here?' I asked. 'And what for?'

"'Oh! He's supposed to have been in terror for his soul, and that he rushed here to get absolution, which, of course, was impossible.'

"'But tell me,' I said. 'Did he come here alone, or how?'

"'Well, you know, after the murder they ransacked the Archbishop's house and stables: and it is said that this man got one of the fastest horses and rode like a madman, not knowing where he was going and that he dashed into the village, and into the church where the priest was: and then afterwards, mounted again and rode off. The priest, too, is buried in the chancel, somewhere, I believe. You see it's a very vague and improbable story. At the Gatehouse at Malling, too, you know, they say that one of the knights slept there the night after the murder.'

"I said nothing more; but I suppose I looked strange, because my friend began to look at me with some anxiety, and then ordered me off to bed: so I took my candle and went.

"Now," said the priest, turning to me, "that is the story. I need not say that I have thought about it a great deal ever since: and there are only two theories which appear to me credible, and two others, which would no doubt be suggested, which appear to me incredible.

"First, you may say that I was obviously unwell: my previous depression and dreaming showed that, and therefore that I dreamed the whole thing. If you wish to think that — well, you must think it.

"Secondly, you may say, with the Psychical Research Society, that the whole thing was transmitted from my friend's brain to mine; that his was in an energetic, and mine in a passive state, or something of the kind.

"These two theories would be called 'scientific,' which term means that they are not a hair's breadth in advance of the facts with which the intellect, a poor instrument at the best, is capable of dealing. And these two 'scientific' theories create in their turn a new brood of insoluble difficulties.

"Or you may take your stand upon the spiritual world, and use the faculties which God has given you for dealing with it, and then you will no longer be helplessly puzzled, and your intellect will no longer overstrain itself at a task for which it was never made. And you may say, I think, that you prefer one of two theories.

"First, that human emotion has a power of influencing or saturating inanimate nature. Of course this is only the old familiar sacramental principle of all creation. The expressions of your face, for instance, caused by the shifting of the chemical particles of which it is composed, vary with your varying emotions. Thus we might say that the violent passions of hatred, anger, terror, remorse, of this poor murderer, seven hundred years ago, combined to make a potent spiritual fluid that bit so deep into the very place where it was all poured out, that under certain circumstances it is reproduced. A phonograph, for example, is a very coarse parallel, in which the vibrations of sound translate themselves first into terms of wax, and then reemerge again as vibrations when certain conditions are fulfilled.

"Or, secondly, you may be old-fashioned and simple, and say that by some law, vast and inexorable, beyond our perception, the personal spirit of the very man is chained to the place, and forced to expiate his sin again and again, year by year, by attempting to express his grief and to seek forgiveness, without the possibility of receiving it. Of course we do not know who he was; whether one of the knights who afterwards did receive absolution, which possibly was not ratified by God; or one of the men-at-arms who assisted, and who, as an anonymous chronicle says, '*sine confessione et viatico sutito rapti sunt*'

"There is nothing materialistic, I think, in believing that spiritual beings may be bound to express themselves within limits of time and space; and that inanimate nature, as well as animate, may be the vehicles of the unseen. Arguments against such possibilities have surely, once for all, been silenced, for Christians at any rate, by the Incarnation and the Sacramental system, of which the whole principle is that the Infinite and Eternal did once, and does still, express Itself under forms of inanimate nature, in terms of time and space.

"With regard to another point, perhaps I need not remind you that a thunderstorm broke over Canterbury on the day and hour of the actual murder of the Archbishop."

The Sorrows of the World

". . . quell' ombre orando, andavan sotto il pondo simile a quel
che talvolta si sogna, disparmente angosciate tutte a tondo e lasse
su per la prima cornice, purganto le caligine del mondo."

Il Purgatorio.

A s the days went on I became more reassured about my
friend. Parker told me there was an improvement since I
had come: and the shadow in his eyes seemed a little lightened. On
Christmas Eve the Rector called, and they were shut up together in
the chapel for an hour after tea; and the old man, I suppose, made
his confession. He seemed brighter than ever that evening, and told
me story after story after dinner, old tales of when he was a child.

On Christmas morning he celebrated the Holy Mysteries as usual
in the chapel, and I received the Communion at his hands. We went
to church in the brougham, and that was the last time the old priest
was seen in public. There was intense curiosity about him in the
village, as well as the greatest reverence and love for him, and I
noticed a ripple of interest along the benches as we passed up to
the Hall pew.

On the evening of Christmas Day he had provided a Christmas
tree in the servants' hall; but we only looked in for a moment when
the shouting was at its loudest, and he nodded at a child or two
who caught sight of him, and I saw his whole face kindle with joy
and tenderness, and then we went back to the fire in the sitting
room.

The morning of St. John's Day broke dark and heavy. We had to
have candles at breakfast, and the old man seemed curiously
changed and depressed again. He hardly spoke at all, and looked at
me almost resentfully, like an overwrought child, when I failed to

blow out the spirit lamp at the first attempt.

All day long the gloom outside seemed to gather, the sun went down in a pale sky barred with indigo, and the wind began to rise.

The old man, after a word or two, went to his room soon after dinner, and I understood from Parker, who presently came in, that the master was exceedingly sorry for his discourtesy, but that he did not feel equal to conversation, and intended to go to bed early, and that he would be obliged if I could manage to amuse myself alone that evening. But I too went upstairs early, feeling a little uneasy.

On the top landing of the north end of the house there are three doors: the central one is the chapel door; that on the right, approached by two little steep steps of its own, was the priest's room; that on the left opposite was my own room. As I went in, I noticed that a light shone from under the chapel door, and that his own door was wide open, showing the flickering light of the fire within. As I paused I saw Parker pass across the doorway, and called to him in a low voice.

"Yes, sir; he's fairly well, I think," he answered to my inquiry. "He is in the chapel just now, and is coming to bed directly. He told me just now, sir, too, to ask whether you would serve him tomorrow morning."

"Certainly," I said; "but are you sure he ought to get up? He has not been well all day."

"Well, sir," said Parker; "I will do my best to persuade him to stay in bed, and will let you know if I succeed, but I doubt whether the master will be persuaded."

As I crossed outside the chapel door to go to my own room I heard a murmur from within, with a word or two which I cannot write down.

Before I was in bed I heard the chapel door open, and footsteps go up the little steps opposite, and the door close. Presently it opened again; and then a tap at my door.

"It's only me, sir," said Parker's voice. "May I speak to you a moment?" and then he came in with a candle in his hand.

"I'm not easy about him, sir," he said. "But he won't let me sleep in his room, as I asked. I've come to ask you whether you will let me lie down on your sofa. I don't like to leave him. My own room is at the other end of the house. Excuse me, sir, if I've asked what I shouldn't. But I don't like to sleep on the landing for fear he should look out and see me, and be displeased."

Of course I assented, almost eagerly, for I felt a strange discomfort and loneliness myself.

Parker went noiselessly downstairs and got a rug or two and a pillow, and then, with many apologies, lay down on the sofa near the window. My bed stood at the other end of the long narrow room under the sloping side of the roof. I blew the candles out presently, and the room was in darkness.

I could not sleep at first. I was anxious for my friend, and I lay and listened for the slightest sound from the landing. But Parker's face, as I had seen it as he had stood with the candle in his hand, reassured me that he too would be on the watch. The wind had half died down again. Only there came gusts from time to time that shook the leaded windows. Gradually I began to doze, then I suppose I dropped off to sleep, and I dreamed.

In my dream I knew that I was still in my room, lying on my bed, but the room seemed illuminated with a light whose source I could not imagine. The curtains, I thought, were no longer drawn over the windows, but looped back, and the light from my room fell distinctly upon the panes. I thought I was sitting up in bed watching for something at the window, something which would terrify me when it came. And then as I watched there came a gust of wind, and lashed, to judge by the sound, a big spray of ivy across the outside. Then again it came, and again, but the sound grew more distinct. I could see nothing at the window, but there came that ceaseless patter and tap, like a thousand fingers. Then a dead leaf or two was whirled up, stuck for a moment on the glass, and whirled away again. It seemed to me that the ivy spray and the leaves were clamoring to be admitted into shelter from that wild wind outside. I grew terrified at their insistence, and tried in my dream to call to Parker, whom I fancied to be still in the room, and in the struggle awoke, and the room was dark. No; as I looked about me it was not quite dark. There lay across the floor an oblong patch of light from the door. I gradually realized that the door was open; there came a draft round the corner at the foot of my bed. I sat up and called gently to Parker. But there was no answer. I got out of bed noiselessly, and went across the floor to where I saw the dim outlines of the sofa. As I drew near I stumbled over a rug, and then felt the pillow, also on the floor. I put my hands almost instinctively down, and felt that the sofa was still warm, but Parker was gone. Then I looked out of the door. The landing was lit by an oil lamp, and its light fell upon the priest's door. It was almost closed, but I could hear a faint murmur of voices.

I put on my dressing gown and slippers and went out. Almost simultaneously the door opposite opened a little wider, and Parker's face looked out, white and scared. When he saw me, he came swiftly out and down the stairs, beckoning to me; but as we met, a loud high voice came from the priest's room.

"Parker, Parker! Tell him to come in — at once — at once. Don't leave me.'

"Go in, sir: go in," Parker said, in a loud whisper to me, pushing me towards the door. I went quickly up the two steep steps and entered, Parker close behind me, and I heard him close the door softly.

There was a tall screen on my left, and behind it was the bed, with the head in the corner of the room: a fire was burning near the bed. I came round the screen quickly, and saw the priest sitting up in bed. He wore a tippet over his shoulders and a small skullcap on his head. His eyes were large and bright, and looked at me almost unintelligently. His hands were hidden by the bedclothes. There was a little round table by the head of the bed, on which stood two burning candles in silver candlesticks. I drew up a chair by the table and sat down.

"My old friend," I said, "what is it? Cannot you sleep?"

He made no answer to me directly, but stared past me round the room, and then fixed his eyes at the foot of the bed.

"The sorrows of the world," he said, "and the sorrows under the earth. They come to me now, because I have not understood them, nor wept for them."

And then he drew out his old, thin, knotted hands, and clasped them outside the rug that lay on the outside of the bed. I laid my own hand upon them.

"You have had a greater gift than that," I said. "You have known instead the joys of the world."

He paid no attention to me, but stared mournfully before him, but he did not withdraw his hands.

There came a sudden gust of wind outside; and even in that corner away from the window the candle flames leaned over to one side, and then the chimney behind me sighed suddenly.

The priest unclasped his hands, and my own hand fell suddenly on the coverlet. He stretched out his left hand to the window as it still shook, and pointed at it in silence, glaring over my head as he did so.

Almost instinctively I turned to the long, low window and looked. But the curtains were drawn over it: they were just stirring and heaving in the draft, but there was nothing to be seen. I could hear the pines tossing and sighing like a troubled sea outside.

Then he broke out into a long wild talk, now in a whisper, and now breaking into something like a scream.

Parker came quickly round from the doorway, where he had been waiting out of sight, and stood behind me, anxious and scared. Sometimes I could not hear what the priest said: he muttered to himself: much of it I could not understand: and some of it I cannot bring myself to write down — so sacred was it — so revealing of his soul's inner life hidden with Christ in God.

"The sorrows of the world," he cried again; "they are crying at my window, at the window of a hard old man and a traitorous priest . . . betrayed them with a kiss. . . . Ah! the Holy Innocents who have suffered! Innocents of man and bird and beast and flower; and I went my way or sat at home in the sunshine; and now they come crying to me to pray for them. How little I have prayed!" Then he broke into a torrent of tender prayer for all suffering things. It seemed to me as he prayed as if the wind and the pines were silent. Then he began again:

"Their pale faces look through the glass; no curtains can shut them out. Their thin fingers tap and entreat. . . And I have closed my heart at that door and cannot open it to let them in. . . . There is the face of a dog who has suffered — his teeth are white, but his eyes are glazed and his tongue hangs out. . . . There is a rose with drenched petals — a rose whom I forgot. See how the wind has battered it. . . . The sorrows of the world! . . . There come the souls from under the earth, crying for one to release them and let them go — souls that all men have forgotten, and I, the chief of sinners. . . . I have lived too much in the sweetness of God and forgotten His sorrows."

Then he turned to a crucifix of ebony and silver that hung on the wall at his side, and looked on it silently. And then again he broke into compassionate prayer to the Savior of the world, entreating Him by His Agony and Bloody Sweat, by His Cross and Passion, to remember all suffering things. That prayer that I heard gave me a glimpse into mysteries of which I had not dreamed; mysteries of the unity of Christ and His members, a unity of pain. These great facts, which I thank God I know more of now, stood out in fiery lines against the dark sorrow that seemed to have filled the room from this old man's heart.

Then suddenly he turned to me, and his eyes so searched my own that I looked down, while his words lashed me.

"You, my son," he said, "what have you done to help our Lord and His children? Have you watched or slept? Couldst thou not watch with me one hour? What share have you borne in the Incarnation? Have you believed for those who could not believe, hoped for the despairing, loved and adored for the cold? And if you could not understand nor do this, have you at least welcomed pain that would have made you one with them? Have you even pitied them? Or have you hidden your face for fear you should grieve too much? But what am I that I should find fault?" Then he broke off again into self-reproach.

At this point Parker bent over me and whispered:

"He will die, sir, I think, unless you can get him to be quiet."

The old man overheard, and turned almost fiercely.

"Quiet?" he cried, "when the world is so unquiet! Can I rest, do you think, with those at my window?" Then, with a loud cry, "Ah! They are in the room! They look at me from the air! I cannot bear it." And he covered his face with his old thin hands, and shrank back against the wall.

I got up from my seat, and looked round as I did so. It seemed to my fancy as if there were some strange Presence filling the room. It seemed as I turned as if crowding faces swiftly withdrew themselves over and behind the screen. A picture on the wall overhead lifted and dropped again like a door as if to let something escape. The coverlet, which was a little disarranged by the old man's movement, rippled gently as if someone who had been seated on the bed had risen. I heard Parker, too, behind me draw his breath quickly through his teeth. All this I noticed in a moment; the next I had bent over the bed towards the priest and put my hand on his shoulder. Either he or I was trembling, I felt as I touched him.

"My dear old friend," I said, "cannot you lie down quietly a little? You cannot think how you are distressing us both."

Then I added a word or two, presumptuously, I felt, in the presence of this old man, who knew so much about the Love of God and the Compassion of our Savior.

Presently he withdrew his hands and looked at me.

"Yes, yes," he said; "but you do not understand. I am a priest."

I sat down again. I tried hard to control a great trembling that had seized me. Still he watched me. Then he said more quietly:

"Is it nearly morning?"

"It is not yet twelve o'clock, sir," said Parker's voice steadily behind me.

"Then I must watch and pray a little longer," said the old man. "Joy cometh in the morning."

Then quite quietly he turned and lifted the crucifix from its nail, kissed it and replaced it. Then he put his hands over his face again and remained still.

The wind outside seemed quieter. But whenever it sighed in the chimney or at the window the priest winced a little, as it a sudden pain had touched him.

He was supported by pillows behind his back and head, against which he leaned easily. After a few minutes of silence his hands dropped and clasped themselves on his lap. His eyes were closed, and he seemed breathing steadily. I hoped that he would fall asleep so. But as I turned to whisper to Parker, I suppose I must have made a slight noise, for when I looked at the servant he paid no attention to me, but was looking at his master. I turned back again, and saw the old man's eyes gazing straight at me.

"Yes," he said; "go and sleep; why are you here? Parker, why did you allow him to come?"

"I woke up and came myself," I said. "Parker did not disturb me."

"Well, go back to bed now. You will serve me in the morning?"

I tried to say something about his not being fit to get up, but he waved it aside.

"You cannot understand," he said quietly. "That is my one hope and escape. Joy cometh in the morning. There are many souls here and elsewhere that are waiting for that joy, and I must not disappoint them. And I too," he added softly, "I too look for that joy. Go now, and we will meet in the morning." And he smiled at me so gently that I got up and went, feeling comforted.

After I had been in bed a little while, I heard the priest's door open and close again, and then Parker tapped at my open door and came in.

"I have left him quiet, sir. I do not think he will sleep, but he would not let me stay."

"Have you ever seen him like this before?" I asked.

"Never quite like this, sir," he said; and as I looked at the old servant I saw that his eyes were bright with tears, and his lips twitching.

"Well," I said, "we have both heard strange things tonight. Your master whom you love is in the hands of God."

The old servant's face broke into lines of sorrow; and then the tears ran down his face.

"Excuse me, sir," he said, "I am not quite myself. Shall I put the candle out, sir?" Then he lay down on the sofa.

"One word more, Parker. You will wake me if you hear anything more. And anyhow you will call me at seven if I should be asleep."

"Certainly, sir," answered Parker's voice from the darkness.

I slept and woke often that night. Each time I woke I went quietly to the door and looked across the landing and listened. Each time I was not so quiet but that Parker heard me and was by me as I looked, and each time there was a line of light under the priest's door; and once or twice a murmur of one voice at least from the room.

Towards morning I fell into a sound sleep, and awoke to find Parker arranging my clothes and setting ready my bath. The rugs and the pillow were gone from the sofa, and there was no sign on the servant's face that anything unusual had happened during the night.

"How is he?" I asked quickly. "Have you seen him?"

"Yes, sir," said Parker; "he is dressing now, and will be ready at half-past seven. It is a little before seven now, sir."

"But how is he?" I asked again.

"I scarcely know, sir," answered Parker. "He does not seem ill, but he is very silent again this morning, sir."

Then, after a pause, "Is there anything I can do for you, sir?"

"There is nothing more, thank you," I said, and he left the room.

I got up presently and dressed. The morning was still dark, and I dressed by candlelight When I drew the curtains back the sky had just begun to glimmer in the reflected dawn from the other side of the house; but it was too dark to see to read except by artificial light.

I went out on to the landing, paused a moment, and heard a footstep in the priest's room. Then I opened the door of the oratory and went in.

In the Morning

"At the end of woe suddenly our eyes shall be opened, and in clearness of light our sight shall be full: which light is God, our Maker and Holy Ghost, in Christ Jesus our Savior."

Mother Julian

The oratory is a little room, whitewashed, crossed by oaken beams on the walls. The window is opposite the door; and the altar stands to the left. There is a bench or two on the right.

When I entered on this morning the tapers were lighted, the vestments laid out upon the altar, and all prepared. I went across and knelt by the window. Presently I heard the priest's door open, and in a moment more he came in, followed by Parker, who closed the door behind him and came and knelt at the bench. I looked eagerly at the old man's face; it was white and tired-looking, and the eyebrows seemed to droop more than ever, but it was a quiet face. It was only for an instant that I saw it, for he turned to the altar and began to vest: and then when he was ready he began.

It was strange to hear that voice, which had rung with such intensity of pain so few hours before, now subdued and controlled; and to watch the orderly movements of those hands that had twisted and gesticulated with such terrible appeal. I felt that Parker too was watching with a close and awful interest what we both half feared would be a shocking climax to the scenes of the night before, but which we half hoped too would recall and quiet that troubled spirit.

Dawn was now beginning to shine on the western sky. There was a tall holly tree that rose nearly to the level of the window. As I looked out for a moment my eye was caught by the outline of a bird, faintly seen, sitting among the upper branches.

Now I will only mention one incident that took place. I was in such a strange and disordered state of mind that I scarcely now can remember certainly anything but this. As the Priest's Communion drew near there came a sudden soft blow against the window panes. . . .

When the priest began to unvest, I left the chapel and went downstairs to await him in the breakfast room. But as he did not come, I went outside the house for a few minutes, and presently found myself below the chapel window. It seemed to me that I was in a dream — the very earth I trod on seemed unreal. I was unable to think connectedly. The scene in the chapel seemed to stand out vividly. It seemed to me as if in some sense it were a climax, but of what nature, whether triumphant or full of doom, I could not tell.

As I stood there, perplexed, downcast, in the growing glimmer of the day, my eyes fell upon a small rumpled heap at my feet, and looking closer I saw it was the body of a thrush; it was still limp and warm, and as I lifted it I remembered the sudden blow against the window panes. But as I still stood, utterly distracted, the chapel window was thrown open, and Parker's face looked out as I gazed up. He beckoned to me furiously and withdrew, leaving the window swinging.

I laid the thrush under a bush at the corner of the house as I ran round, and came in quickly and up the stairs. Parker met me on the landing.

"He just reeled and fell, sir," he said, "up the stairs into his room. I've laid him on the bed, and must get down to the stables to send for the doctor. Will you stay with him, sir, till I come back?" And without waiting for an answer he was gone.

That evening I was still sitting by my friend's side. I had food brought up to my room during the day, but except for those short intervals was with him continually. The doctor had come and gone. All that he could tell us was that the old man had had a seizure of some kind, and he had looked grave when I told him of the events of the night before.

"His age is against him, too," the doctor had said; "I cannot say what will happen."

And then he had given directions, and had left, promising to return again, at any rate the next morning.

I had been trying to read with a shaded lamp, looking from time to time at the figure of the old man on the bed, as he lay white and quiet, with his eyes closed, as he had lain all day.

At about six o'clock, I had just glanced at my watch, when a slight movement made me turn to the bed again, and I could see in the dim light that his eyes were open and fixed upon me, but all the pain was gone out of them, and they were a child's eyes again. I rose and went to his side, and sat down in the same chair that I had occupied the night before. Immediately I had sat down he put out his hand, and I took it and held it. His eyes smiled at me, and then he spoke, very slowly, with long pauses.

"Well," he said, "you have been with me and have seen and heard, last night and this morning; but it is all ended, and the valley is lightening again at its eastern end where the sun rises. So it was not all dreams and fancies — those old stories that you bore with so patiently to please me. Now tell me what you heard and saw. Did you see them all in the room last night? And — and —" his eyes grew wide and insistent — "what did you see this morning?"

Now the doctor had told me that he must not be over-excited, but soothed; and honestly enough, though some who may read this may not agree with me, I thought it was better to speak plainly of those things so strange to you and me, but so dear and familiar to him. And so I told him all I had heard and seen.

"Ah!" he said when I had finished, "then we were not quite as one. But still you saw and heard more than most men. Now will you hear one more story? I will not tell you all I saw last night, because the Lord has been gracious to me, and is rising with healing in His wings on me and on many other poor creatures. But the wounds are aching still, and if you will spare me, I will not speak much of the shadows of last night, but only of the joys that came in the morning. Will you hear it?"

"My dear old friend," I said, "are you sure it will not be too much for you?"

He shook his head; and then, still holding my hand in his, his fingers tightening and relaxing as he told his tale, with many pauses and efforts, he began:

"Last night the sorrows of death came to me," he said, "and all the blood and agony and desolation of the whole world seemed to be round me. And I have had so little sorrow in my life that I was ill prepared to meet them. Our Lord has always shown me such grace and given me so much joy. But He warned me again and again this autumn. That was why I spoke to you as I did when you came before Christmas.

"Well, last night, all this came to me. And it seemed as if I were partly responsible. Years ago I was set apart as a priest to stand between the dead and the living. It was meant that I should be the meeting place, as every priest must be, of creation's need and God's grace — as every Christian must be in his station. That is what intercession and the Holy Sacrifice both signify and effect. The two tides of need and fulfillment must meet in a priest's heart. But all my life I have known much of fulfillment and little of need. Last night the first was almost withdrawn, and the second deepened almost beyond bearing. But I knew, as I told you last night, that with the morning would come peace — that I should be able to carry up the burden laid on me, and make it one with Him on Whom the iniquities of us all are laid. But I need not say more of that now. This morning when I went to the altar a lull had come in the storm. But it was all in my heart still. I felt sure that I should have the clear vision once more: and as I lifted up the Body of our Lord, it came.

"As I lifted It up It disappeared; as those tell us who look in crystals. And this is what I saw. I do not know how long I saw it, it seemed as if time stood still, but you told me there was no perceptible pause. Well," — and the old man raised himself slightly in the bed — "between my hands I saw a long slope running as it seemed from me downhill. On the nearer higher end of the slope were men going to and fro, and I knew they needed something — and yet many of them did not seem to know it themselves but they were all in need. One there was who walked quickly, clenching and unclenching his hands, and I knew he fought with sin. And there was a woman with a dead child across her knees; and there was a blind child crying in a corner.

"Then further down the slope were wounded creatures of all kinds, and lonely beasts seeking a place to die, and the very grass of the field seemed to be in sorrow, and there were blind sea creatures gasping. They were not small, as you might think, but I saw them as if I looked through a hole in a wall.

"And they stretched down, rank on rank, heaving and striving, men and beasts warring and trampling down the flowers. There was a thrush I saw, too, shivering in a tree; and the thought of the story I have told you came to my mind, and there were a thousand things that I forget.

"Now when I saw all this my hands trembled, but what I saw did not tremble, so I knew that it was real. And then very far away and faint at the foot of the slope was a level silvery mist, like a sea-fog, with delicate currents and lines, now swift and piercing, now slow; and in the mist moved faces; but I could not distinguish the features. And these were the souls that waited until their sins should be done away.

"And then with something like terror I remembered that I held in my hands the Body of the Lord. And I was puzzled and distracted, but I knelt to adore, and as I lowered the Holy Thing, the clouds closed and the light died out. And it may be that I was cowardly — and I think God will pardon an old man for whom the light was too strong — but when I consecrated the chalice, I dared not look at it. At the Communion, too, I closed my eyes again." The old man paused a moment and then continued. "I heard no sound such as you describe. As I unvested and went to my room I was still perplexed at what I had seen, and could not understand it, and then on a sudden I understood it, and it was then I suppose that I fell down."

There was a silence for a moment: then I answered.

"I cannot understand even now."

The priest smiled at me, and his hand closed again on mine.

"I think there is no need for me to tell you that. It will be plain to you soon. Remember what it was that I saw, and where I saw it, and all will be easy.

"You can leave me now for a little," he went on. "I am perfectly free from pain, and I wish to think. Would you send Parker to me in about an hour's time?" And then, as I went towards the door, he added:

"One word more. I had forgotten something. I have yet one more clear vision to see before I die. I have seen, you remember, what you too have seen, how all things need God; but there is yet one more thing to see which will make all plain, and I think you can guess what that is. . And I pray that you will be with me when I see it."

Then I turned and went quietly out.

The Expected Guest

"Jhesu! Jhesu! Esto michi, Jhesu!"

Old Prayer

As day after day went by and the old man seemed no worse, I began to have hopes that he might recover, but the doctor discouraged me.

"At the best," he said, "he may just linger on. But I do not think the end is far off. You must remember he is an old man." And so at last the end came.

During these days, since Parker was of course too much occupied with his master, a boy waited on me. On the last evening, as the boy came in for the second time at dinner, he looked white and frightened.

"What is it?" I asked.

"We don't like it, sir, in the servants' hall. Two children ran in just now and said they had seen something, and we are all upset, sir. The maids are crying."

"What was it the children thought they saw?" I asked. The boy hesitated.

"Tell me," I repeated.

The boy put down the dish he held and came closer to me.

"They say they saw the master himself, sir, on the front lawn, at the gate."

"Where were the children?" I asked.

"Passing round from the house, sir, in front, under the chestnut. They had been sent by the Rector to inquire."

I got up from the table.

"Where are they?" I asked.

"In the servants' hall, sir."

"Bring them into the sitting room." And I followed him out and waited. Presently the swing door opened and the children looked in. Behind them were the pale faces of the servants, whispering and staring.

"Come in," I said to the children, "and sit down. Don't be afraid."

They came timidly in, evidently very much frightened. The door closed behind them.

This was their story.

They had been to the house to inquire how the old man was, and were returning to the Rectory. But they had hardly started, in fact had only just reached the chestnut tree in front of the house, when both of them, who were looking towards the lighted windows, had seen quite plainly the figure of the old priest standing just inside the gate. He was bareheaded, they said, dressed in black, but they could only see his head and shoulders over the bank, as the road is a little lower than the grass which borders on it and runs up to the gate. He seemed, they said, to be looking out for someone. When I asked them how they could possibly see anyone at that distance on such a dark night, they had no sort of explanation; they could only repeat that they did see him quite plainly. At last I took them out myself, and made them point out to me the place where they had seen it; but, as I expected, all was dark, and we could not even make out the white balls on the pedestals. I took them on to the end of the drive, as they still seemed upset; and they told me there that they would not be frightened to go the rest of the way alone. Fortunately, however, as we waited a man passed in the direction of the village, and he consented to see them as far as the Rectory gate.

When I entered the house again the maids with the boy were standing in the hall. They looked eagerly towards the door as I opened it, and one of them cried out.

"What is it now?" I asked. One of the elder servants answered:

"Oh sir, the master's worse. Parker's afraid he's going. He's just run downstairs for you, sir; and now he's gone back."

I did not wait to hear any more, but pushed past them, through the sitting room, and ran upstairs.

The door of the old man's room was open, and I heard faint sounds from within. I went straight in without knocking, and turned the corner of the screen.

Parker, who was kneeling by the bed, supporting his master in his arms, turned his head as I came in sight, and made a gesture with it. I came close up.

"He's going fast, sir, I'm afraid," he whispered.

The old man was sitting up in bed looking quite straight before him. His lips were slightly parted; and his eyes were full of expectancy. He kept lifting his hands gently, half opening them with a welcoming movement, and then letting them fall. Now he leaned gently forward, as if to meet something with his hands extended, then sinking a little back upon Parker's arm. He paid no attention to me, and it seemed as if his eyes were focused to an almost infinite distance.

I too knelt down by the bed and waited watching him. Then there came soft footsteps at the door, but it was not for that he waited. Then a whispering and a sobbing: and I knew that the servants were gathering outside.

Still he waited for that which he knew would come before he died. And the expectancy deepened in his eyes to an almost terrible intensity; and it was the expectancy that feared no disappointment. It was perfectly still outside, the servants were quiet now, and the old man's breathing was inaudible. Once I heard the far-off bark of a dog away somewhere in the village.

As I watched his face I saw how wrinkles covered it, the corners of his eyes and his forehead were deeply furrowed, and the lines deepened and shifted as his face worked. And then suddenly he cried out: "He is coming, my son, He is coming far away." And then silence.

I heard a sudden movement outside and then stillness again. Then a maid broke out into sobbing: and I heard footsteps, and then the door of my room across the landing open and shut: and the sobbing ceased. But the old man paid no heed. Then suddenly he cried out again:

"Behold He stands at the door and knocks."

He made an indescribable gesture with his hands. Then I was startled, for there came a loud pealing at the bell downstairs.

Parker whispered to me to send one of the servants downstairs: and I went to the door for an instant and told the boy to go: then I came back. The boy's footsteps died away down the staircase. I knelt down again by the bed.

Then once more the old man cried out:

"He is coming, my son. He is here;" and then, "Look!"

As he said this across his face there came an extraordinary smile; for one moment, as I started up and looked, his face was that of a child, the wrinkles seemed suddenly erased, and a great rosy flush swept from forehead to mouth, and his eyes shone like stars. I noticed too, even at this moment, for I was almost facing him as I sprang up, that the focus of his eyes was contracted to a point at the foot of his bed where the screen stood.

Then he fell back; and Parker laid him gently down.

A moment after footsteps came up the stairs: and the boy whispered from the doorway that the Rector had come.

The End.

www.ingramcontent.com/pod-product-compliance
Lightning Source LLC
Chambersburg PA
CBHW030346030726
47499CB00003B/924

* 9 780972 982160 *